I0536208

IT'S HER FAULT AND THE OTHER FRANK

IT'S HER FAULT AND THE OTHER FRANK

TONY GLEESON

Personal Crimes Mysteries, Vol. 2

WILDSIDE PRESS

To Annie, who never left

Copyright © 2019 by Tony Gleeson.
Published by Wildside Press LLC.
www.wildsidepress.com

CONTENTS

IT'S HER FAULT

ONE

It all began when Marlon Morrison refused to abandon his meatball marinara sandwich.

"Hey Frank," he called across his desk. "Do me a favor and take this call for me?" Even as he plunged the meatball hero into his gaping mouth with his left hand, he held out a pink phone slip with his right.

It was not surprising to Frank Vandegraf that his colleague, Detective Morrison, wanted to pass off still another chore on someone else. There was a running joke in the Personal Crimes Unit, that Morrison, when thanked for some favor or other, was fond of saying, "It was the very least I could do," and that was absolutely what he always did, the very least he could.

Frank, who had been trying to walk past Marlon's desk without calling attention to himself, sighed resignedly and reached out for the slip. What the hell, he figured. He was, if not free, at least relatively unencumbered at the moment, as much as anybody in the unit ever was. Why not.

"Some professor says his wife is trying to kill him," Morrison said with a mouth full of meatball and Parmesan cheese.

Frank gave the phone slip a quick scan.

"Somewhere up in the hills," Morrison added before taking another bite. The marinara sauce was dripping off the sandwich onto the paper wrapper underneath. It smelled good. Frank made a note to grab a bite while he was out.

"I owe you one, Frank," Marlon called to his back as he departed. Marlon owed a lot of guys one. He owed most of them more than one. Frank wasn't going to hold his breath waiting to get reimbursed.

* * * *

The hills that rose along the eastern side of the city were a twenty minute drive from the station, which no doubt partly accounted for Marlon's reluctance to take the call, but it was also a nice jaunt through some of the better neighborhoods. Frank judged that he could use a little cheering up, so he was actually whistling as he grabbed his car keys from his desk and headed out the door.

Developers had taken full advantage of the views afforded from the hillside to the harbor and coast off to the west. Further to the north, as the hills got higher, were expensive one-family hillside homes, but Frank's destination was the condominium district, where a line of identical, trendily-designed buildings rose into the sky. The district had been officially named Scenic Hills by the developers but the name had never stuck and most still simply referred to the area as the Hills.

Professor Maurice Hesterberg lived near the top floor of such a building.

"Thank you for coming, Detective Vandegraf," Hesterberg was saying as he sat next to him on his balcony. It was a glorious sunny day, a good breeze making the air crystal clear, and they could see the ocean in the distance right to the horizon.

He rattled the ice cubes in his glass of iced tea. "You're sure I can't get you something?"

"Thanks, no," Frank replied. He had pulled a beat-up notebook out of his pocket and opened it to the next available page. "Now tell me, Mr. Hesterberg..."

"Doctor," Hesterberg interrupted.

"Excuse me?"

"That's Doctor Hesterberg."

"Doctor Hesterberg. All right..."

"I know, it seems pretentious, doesn't it?" He spoke in a clipped but precise manner, more than a little fussy and self-conscious. Frank could see it was going to get annoying soon enough.

"Not a problem, Doctor...now..."

"But, you see, I worked very, very hard to earn that title. While I was working on my Master's and PhD, I also worked full time as an electrician."

"Do tell."

"Crawled around under houses, in between walls. Got shocked

more than a few times. Fell out of a few houses. Not an easy way to get through school."

It did not sound, Frank reflected silently, that the Doctor was very good at being an electrician. It was probably a good thing that he had gone into academia.

"So you see, I kind of feel I deserve that title of respect. Sometimes people tell me they think only medical doctors deserve to be called Doctor. I tell them, respectfully, that's rubbish."

Respectfully indeed, Frank reflected.

"Whatever you say, Doctor Hesterberg. I have no trouble with calling you that. Now you reported that you think someone is trying to kill you?"

"My wife, that's correct. My estranged wife, to be precise."

Which explained, Frank mused, why so far there seemed to be no sign of a female presence in this condo. Of course he couldn't have unerringly made that judgment without having yet seen the bedroom and the bathroom, but a detective of a certain number of years just picked up on some things intuitively.

"Your wife does not live here then, sir?"

"No, we have been separated for some time now. She lives in an apartment on the other side of town."

"Your wife's name is...?"

"Margo. Margo Hesterberg. We are still officially married." Hesterberg sighed deeply, looking out at the view. "Hopefully not for too much longer."

"So tell me, why do you think Margo is trying to kill you, uh, Doctor?"

"Well, for one thing, she poisoned my dog. For another thing, she's threatened me. And she's tried to break into my condominium."

"Poisoned your dog?"

"Yes. I found my Schnauzer, Thomas Mann, dead one evening when I returned home. Lying there by his food dish, by the kitchen window over there, under those Venetian blinds." He pointed through the open balcony door into the apartment.

"Thomas Mann."

"That's his name, yes. After the German novelist."

"I've heard of him, thank you. Wrote 'Death in Venice' I believe?" Frank resisted the urge to pursue the apparent irony any further.

"I am suitably impressed, Detective. You're a reader then."

Frank waved a hand. "He was poisoned, you're sure? The dog, I mean, not the writer."

"My veterinarian did an autopsy and confirmed it. I also brought the food dish to him and he found traces of rat poison in it."

"So someone had come into your home and left poison for Thomas—I mean, your dog."

"Yes." Hesterberg nodded vigorously, jaw set. "I duly reported it to the police but no action was ever taken."

Frank scribbled rapidly into his notebook. "You feel this was done by your wife and it was part of an ongoing threat directed at you."

"No question in my mind about it."

"And why do you feel it was your wife who broke into your home and killed your dog?"

"Because she hated him. She said I loved Thomas Mann more than I did her."

"There were signs of her breaking in? Something to lead you to conclude it had to be her?"

"I don't know what it would look like if someone tampered with the lock. I surmise she had a key."

"To your knowledge did she have a key?"

"No. I changed the locks when she left. But somehow she must have gotten one."

"Let's come back to that in a moment, Doctor. Tell me some more about the perceived threats Margo made on your life."

"She would call me at all hours of the night, wake me up, and rave at me. Accuse me of all sorts of bizarre perfidy. More than once she said she was going to make sure I couldn't cause her any more trouble."

"Trouble."

"Yes, that was the word she used: 'trouble.' Several times she said that."

"What kind of trouble did she think you were causing her?"

Hesterberg shrugged and dramatically opened his eyes wide. He had thick dark wiry eyebrows and a beard to match. Combined with his self-conscious manner, the effect was heavy on the drama.

"I never got that straight, Detective. She was increasingly irrational. All I know is that she made clear-cut threats to my well-being in her late-night telephone rants."

"Is there any record of these calls? Did you happen to tape any of these, for example?"

"My God no," Hesterberg replied. "Now I wish I had taken steps to do so."

"Did your wife specifically and expressly say she was going to try to kill you?"

Hesterberg shook his head in frustration. "I can't recall specifically, no, but her meaning was clear."

"She said, maybe, she was going to take you out? Remove you from the scene? Eliminate you? Something like that?"

"Conceivably. I don't remember exactly. The woman has been irrational."

"Did these calls start before or after you found your dog poisoned?"

Hesterberg considered this. "It was around the same time; I believe she began disturbing me just before I found poor Thomas Mann's body."

"Did you confront her with this, ask her if she had done it?"

"One night I did, yes. She did not confirm it, but neither did she outright deny it. She rather laughed. The night conversations were unhinged, you have to understand, very disturbing. They were not the most coherent. I have to admit I found myself drawn into her madness and often responded emotionally. Not to mention she always woke me so I wasn't at my best to begin with."

"When did you last speak with your wife, Doctor?"

"It's been a few days now. Two or three. She hasn't called. There's been no word or contact from her. That's why I'm really worried now."

Frank paused in his writing and looked up. "Excuse me? You're really worried now because...?"

"It's the calm before the storm, of course," Hesterberg intoned dramatically. "She's stopped calling me because she's up to something. I can feel it. So I knew it was time to call the police."

The remainder of the interview was not much more helpful. Frank ascertained that Hesterberg had been a tenured English professor at the nearby State University for many years, and even headed the department for a while. At age 65 he was currently semi-retired, reluctant to totally give up his life's work, teaching only two full time upper division courses and acting as advisor for a doctoral candidate. The rest of his time was devoted to a book he was writing on twentieth century German literary movements, and apparently to long walks and an occasional visit to a local bar for a few Cognacs with one or two fellow academics.

He and Margo had been married for about a quarter of a century and had, in his words, grown increasingly apart from one another over the past few years. Hesterberg attributed much of their marital discord to what he termed Margo's ongoing "descent into madness"—becoming ever more paranoid, suspicious, and withdrawn. She was, he said, jealous of any time or energy he spent with anyone else or anything else. She suspected his tavern companions, his long walks, even his dog.

He did have to admit, she had never once committed a violent act or even shown any tendencies to violence, but she had grown increasingly emotional and irrational. Finally the confrontation erupted that resulted in her decision to leave him. She had rented an apartment near her sister, her last surviving relative. Hesterberg figured that once a divorce had been effected, they would sell the condo, which was still joint property, and divide the proceeds.

Frank wondered why Margo had left rather than Hesterberg himself. It was explained that she had made that judgment herself; she wanted nothing more to do with the place where they had spent so much time together. The memories, she said, were not pleasant.

"So let me make sure I've got the actual facts here straight," Frank summed up as he prepared to leave, tucking his notebook into his inner sport coat pocket. "You suspect that your wife plans to kill you. She's made no specific statement to that effect, to you or to anyone else in your knowledge. You believe she entered your condo illicitly and poisoned your dog, but you have no concrete proof of either of these things."

"My feelings are strong on this, Detective. I am totally convinced it is she and that is her plan, yes." Hesterberg seemed to see no difficulty in this view. "So what are you going to do about it?"

"I'm afraid my options are a bit limited legally here, sir. Frankly, your feelings by themselves are not much for me as a basis for action. I'm going to go have a talk with her for starters. Then I'll see where that takes me."

"Are you going to provide me police protection?" Hesterberg demanded.

Frank rubbed the back of his neck. "I don't know that I've got enough to be able to get that for you, but I'll look into it. If there was just something more clear-cut..."

"She's a deranged woman. I've never known her to be specifically violent, I told you that, but there's something different about her of late. She's become frighteningly unpredictable. I'm absolutely convinced she is dangerous."

The address Frank had been given for Margo was an older but still highly respectable neighborhood, where brick predominated: four- and five-story apartment buildings and some two-story row houses along tree-lined streets. There were actually people on the streets, walking dogs, riding bikes. Kids were playing.

Frank considered that he would have opted for a neighborhood like this over the condos any time.

Margo lived in a garden apartment to the rear in a low building. Frank rang the number on the intercom several times but received no answer. Finally he rang the on-premises superintendent, who luckily was home and buzzed him in. Another nice perk, he mused, of an older neighborhood like this one.

The building was tended by a husband and wife who lived in the basement; the wife happened to be the one who was present to greet Frank. She was dressed in slacks and sweatshirt, a robust, no-nonsense looking type, maybe fifty, who stood at her open door with her arms crossed as Frank produced his badge and ID and mentioned the garden apartment.

"Looking for Miz Hesterberg," she observed.

"Yes, ma'am. She isn't answering the bell. Have you seen her recently?"

"Can't say as I have," Super Lady replied. "What's this about?"

"Just routine, I need to talk with her. Any idea when she might be home?"

"She usually *is* home. Doesn't go out all that much, maybe to do shopping or visit her sister down the street."

"Any chance she's home and just not answering the bell?"

Super Lady shrugged. "You're welcome to go knock on her door and see."

Frank did just that, hiking up the steps and down the hall to the rear apartment. He knocked several times and called out "Mrs. Hesterberg?" but there was no reply. He went back to the superintendents' apartment and knocked on the door. Super Lady threw it open.

"If we're going to get to be this friendly," she said dryly, "you might as well know my name's Judy."

"Sorry to bother you again, uh, Judy. I was just wondering if you know Margo's sister, her name, maybe her exact address?"

"Her sister's name is Monica. She lives around the corner." She rattled off an address. Frank fumbled for a pencil and his notebook and wrote it down, thanked her and departed.

Monica Wersching did indeed happen to be at home; she lived in a brick row house, aging but well-maintained, with a cement stoop leading up to the entrance. She promptly answered the doorbell and after inspecting his credentials, invited Frank in.

"So this is about Margo," she said as she led him into a front parlor and motioned for him to have a seat. "Are you finally going to do something, then?"

"Ma'am, excuse me?" Frank said as he sat down in a comfortable leather chair. She sat across from him on her sofa.

"About her husband. About the threats."

The sister apparently knew about the threats? This was interesting but confusing.

"Maybe you better tell me what you're referring to?" He didn't take out his notebook yet, just leaned forward, forearms across his thighs, fingers laced, and stared intently.

"Did she finally contact you? As I've been urging her to do for some time now?"

"No Ma'am. Contact me about what, exactly?"

Monica was a lean, serious-looking woman, perhaps in her late fifties. She returned Frank's gaze earnestly. "About the threats of course! From Max!"

"Max? Who's Max?"

Now Monica was getting irritated. "Her *husband!* MAX!"

"You mean Maurice. Maurice Hesterberg."

"Yes. She always called him Max. Tell me that's why you're here. Please tell me."

"You're telling me that Margo has been receiving threats from her husband, Doctor Hesterberg?"

"And you're telling me that's not why you're here, Detective?" Now Monica looked really perturbed. "So tell me, why *are* you here, then?"

Frank took a deep breath and decided to start over.

He listened, now with his notebook and pencil in hand, as Monica told him the stories her younger sister Margo had shared with her about odd and alarming behavior on the part of her husband since she had moved out.

When she had first found the garden apartment, she had been delighted. She could walk out her back door into a small verdant paradise with a canopy of trees, full bushes, lovely color pots of flowers, and a charming stone walk, all sheltered by ivy-covered brick walls. Since the incidents, she was terrified to be living on a ground floor and was actively searching for a new apartment several stories off the ground with less access from unwanted intruders. She was convinced that her husband had broken into her place several times and had performed what she termed "subtle vandalism" of various sorts.

"She would find things broken," Monica said. "Or missing. Or, strangest of all, mysteriously misplaced, from one location to another inside the apartment. She was sure it was Max, that he was 'Gaslighting' her, as she liked to call it. Are you familiar with that old movie, Detective?"

"A bit before my time, but yes, I've seen it. Ingrid Bergman and Charles Boyer. A classic from the forties. I get her reference. He was trying to convince her she was going mad by manipulating things."

"Margo is quite the film buff. She tells me she prefers the earlier British version, actually. But that's neither here nor there. You understand my point."

"Margo thinks her husband is trying to drive her crazy—or at least make her appear that she's crazy, is that what you're saying?"

"Exactly. She was hesitant to contact the police because she was sure that's just what you *would* think."

Frank caught himself rubbing the back of his neck. He had to stop this habit. Several people had told him that he did it constantly.

"Mrs. Wersching..."

"It's Ms. now, actually," she interrupted. "I'm not partial to being called 'Miss.' My husband passed away some years ago. I readopted my original family name."

"I'm sorry, Ms. Wersching. I've been told that Margo has tended to be a little, well, over-stressed of late and perhaps unduly suspicious. Is it possible that..."

"That she's imagining things? That she's paranoid? Is that why you're here, Detective Vanderbilt?"

"Vandegraf actually," Frank corrected. This was not productive. "Listen, I think I need to speak with Margo herself, directly. She doesn't seem to be at home right now. Do you have any idea when would be a good time for me to catch her?"

"I don't know, I haven't spoken with her in a couple of days myself. She spends a lot of time at home, in her garden. At least she used to. Lately she locks her doors and windows and sits inside and reads or watches DVDs of old films. Let me give her a call."

She got up and walked to a cordless phone on a nearby table. A lot of people were giving up their land lines nowadays, Frank mused. At home, he still liked keeping his.

Monica dialed and waited. Apparently an answering machine or voice mail picked up because she left a short message for Margo to call her back. She hit the OFF button and turned to Frank with a shrug.

"No idea where she might be," she said. "I'll let you know if I hear from her."

Frank stood up and handed her one of his cards, then stopped and sat back down. He asked for, and jotted down Monica's phone number. "If you don't mind, can I just ask you a few more questions about Margo?"

Monica looked somewhat less friendly than she had only shortly before, but she relented and sat down. "Such as?"

"Can you tell me about her marriage to Max—I mean Doctor Hesterberg?"

"She met him when she was a grad student and he was her faculty advisor. He was a rather dashing and romantic sort in those days. He was brilliant and mature, well-traveled and experienced, but he embraced a very youthful life style, the way he dressed and talked, the music he listened to.

"He was very open to the younger culture, loved his students, went drinking with them—probably smoked pot with them too, is my guess. She was considerably his junior in years, of course, maybe fifteen years, naïve and idealistic. Not surprisingly, she became infatuated with him and fell in love."

"They got married, what, twenty years ago?"

"Twenty-five, to be exact. He basically swept her off her feet. She was quite beautiful, full of the love of life. I could see why he was attracted to her. They seemed very happy in those early years."

"You're saying they became less happy with time."

"Gradually, don't people always?"

"I don't know if I'm quite that cynical," Frank allowed, still writing. "But yes, married people do sometimes get disenchanted. But your point is that the marriage was no longer idyllic?"

"More so in recent years. Margo seemed very disturbed by something that was going on. She made comments about finding out that Max wasn't precisely what she had thought he was."

"Any idea what she meant by that?"

"Oh, I pressed her, but she remained cryptic. Would not tell me details."

"Is it possible her husband was having some kind of affair, something like that?"

Monica shrugged slightly. "I never knew or heard of anything like that. Max had settled down after meeting Margo. He seemed to grow up, be more serious. He seemed more interested in his work than, say, in other women. I suppose it's not out of the question. Such things do happen as men grow older and happen to notice their wives are doing the same, don't they?"

She smiled, saw Frank was not going to rise to the bait, and moved on. "I don't entirely know what Margo meant when she started telling me Max wasn't what she had thought he was. She wouldn't elaborate."

"When did she first start telling you things like that?"

Monica thought about that for a while before replying. "Maybe three years ago was when she really began to get agitated."

"Ms. Wersching, please do not take this the wrong way. I have to consider every possibility here. Is it possible your sister was becoming...disturbed in some way...that she was believing things were happening that might not have been?"

Monica shot Frank a glare. "You mean was she going crazy, imagining things? Is that what you're asking?"

"As I said, I've got to consider every possibility here. I don't know any of you."

"Trying to be as fair as I can with you, Detective, Margo was getting more and more...disconcerted, shall we say...on a daily basis over the past few years. She was clearly emotionally upset and progressively allowing it to affect her more. I can't discount that that might have colored her perceptions of things. In fact I was very worried for her state of well-being. But I'm positive that her emotional state was being adversely affected by something very real that had happened, not that the state of mind came first and created something terrible but imagined. I hope that helps because it's the best I can tell you."

"I'm really going to need to talk to Margo in any case," Frank said, standing up. "From what you tell me, she concluded that her husband meant her harm but there was nothing clear cut or specific, no hard evidence to that effect?"

Monica stood up, shaking her head. "Not that I know of. You are really going to need to talk to her. I'll let you know the moment I hear from her. I've been trying to get her to talk to the police for some time now."

As Frank headed for the door, Monica added a final thought. "I do hope that when you do talk with her, you give some credence to her concerns. She's not crazy. And I really don't trust Max."

TWO

In the spare time he could muster, Frank was somewhat of a fan of mysteries. He watched a few cop shows on television and liked a well-done murder mystery novel or movie.

As he sat at his desk and computer, plowing through files and paperwork, typing up reports and struggling through email inquiries, he reflected that in the fictional procedurals, it always seemed as if the cops only had one case at a time to which they could devote their total, undivided attention. That was hardly the true state of affairs for a real detective like himself, he thought. It had been a day and a half now, and he really had not had time to follow up on the strange but unpromising Hesterberg case.

Yesterday Marlon had stopped by his desk to ask how the death threat thing had gone and Frank had been noncommittal, saying only he was tracking down more information. That seemed to have gratified Marlon: he had gauged the whole thing right as a waste of time. Better Frank's than his.

When he found an opportune pause, it occurred to Frank to check back in with Monica Wersching. He punched her number into his aging flip-style mobile phone. She answered after one ring and he identified himself.

"Yes, Detective, I can see on my phone that this call is from the Police Department. Phones do that now."

Frank let that slide. He already knew he was a dinosaur. "Just wanted to see if you've been able to get in touch with Margo."

"Curiously, no, I haven't. Her phone goes right to voice mail every time, day or night. I went over and knocked on her door a few times. I even pulled myself up on her back wall and peered over to see if she was in her garden. No sign of her. In fact I was going to go over and ask her super to let me into the apartment today, just to check."

"Is there someplace she might have gone, taking a vacation or just a respite? Does she ever do that?"

"Rarely. And if she did, she wouldn't go alone. She would have asked me to come along. Certainly at least she'd have told me."

"Does Margo have any friends that she might have gone off with?"

"She has friends but nobody she's kept in touch with recently. Except for me, that is. She's kept her own counsel largely in the past two years or so."

There was nothing Frank could really do to pursue the inquiry until he had been able to speak with Margo, so he felt himself at a standstill. For some reason Margo had decided to clear out for the moment. Somehow Frank didn't think any foul play was involved. At worst she was confused and disoriented and might have wandered off and gotten lost.

"That might be a good idea, Ms. Wersching, to go over and check her apartment again. Please let me know if you're unable to locate her. Maybe it'll be advisable to file a missing persons report."

"Maybe Max got to her, is that what you're thinking?"

Frank hoped she couldn't hear him catching his breath through the phone. "No, no. Not necessarily. But I might be a little concerned that since she was so worried, she would become a little distracted and find herself in unfamiliar territory."

"My sister is not crazy or senile or incompetent, Detective," Monica replied tartly.

"My apologies, that wasn't what I meant to suggest. Please, just let me know after you've been over to her apartment, okay?"

Monica agreed and ended the conversation. Frank regarded the pile of forms in front of him and dove in once again.

It was late in the day when Frank was summoned into the office of his immediate supervisor, Lieutenant Hank Castillo, and handed a phone slip.

"I believe you've already been dealing with this individual," was all Castillo said, as if that were all that needed to be said by way of explanation. Frank looked down at the slip and swore softly under his breath.

"I think you need to get over there, Frank."

* * * *

The body still lay in the entrance hallway where it had fallen. There were personnel from the medical examiner's office and the Scientific Investigation Division lab, bustling around at work, moving economically, skillfully avoiding one another in the tight surroundings. Frank held up the badge he wore on a lanyard for the benefit of the assistant coroner crouching over the corpse. He looked up.

"So what have we got here?"

"Hello, Detective. It seems that he answered his door and whoever was there shot him with a Taser gun. Knocked him down, and apparently killed him. A bit unusual—usually Tasers aren't fatal, but it's not totally unheard of."

He pointed down to the victim's chest. His shirt had been unbuttoned. There were two sets of nasty dark burns in his pectorals. "Conceivably cardiac arrest. More will be revealed. His name is..."

"Yes, I know," interrupted Frank. "Maurice Hesterberg. I'm familiar with him."

He pulled aside one of the uniformed officers on the scene and asked to be brought up to speed. Pending confirmation by autopsy and lab work, it was fairly easy to reconstruct what had probably happened to begin with. Hesterberg had answered the doorbell in his condo, where someone had fired into him the two dart-like electrodes of an electro-shock weapon, probably a Taser gun.

The reconstruction after that became more speculative.

"How long ago?" Frank asked.

"Likely mid-day, early afternoon."

"How was he found?"

"The door was left partly open when the attacker fled. It would seem they never entered further into the apartment, just pulled the darts and wires free and left. Victim's foot partly blocked the door from closing. A neighbor coming down the hall a while later noticed the door ajar and looked in."

Frank jotted notes. "I'll need to talk to that neighbor. Anybody else been in here or seen anything? Neighbors, friends?"

The officer shook his head. "But there was a note."

"A note?"

One of the lab techs crouching on the floor picked up a clear plastic bag between thumb and forefinger of her gloved hand and passed it up to Frank. "It was on his chest. We have photos."

Frank had already pulled on a pair of disposable gloves that he carried with him as a matter of course and he took the bag. There was a regular letter-size piece of paper that had apparently been run through a desktop printer then folded in half. It bore, in large bold type, three simple words:

IT'S HER FAULT

Frank's brain began to process everything, formulate his plan of action. One thing he knew he had to do as soon as possible was to locate Margo Hesterberg. He stepped out of the hallway, found Monica Wersching's number on his phone, and punched the connect to it. He got her voice mail.

"Monica, this is Detective Frank Vandegraf. I need to know if you've found your sister, and in any case, I need to speak with you. Please get back to me as soon as you get this. I don't care how late it is."

He turned back to the uniform and asked a few more questions, ascertained all the details that were available. It appeared that Hesterberg had been home alone; nobody else had apparently even been home on the rest of the floor.

"Where's the neighbor?"

"Two doors down, 1207." He pointed to his left facing the door. "Name's..." he squinted at his own notebook. "Her...Herm...?"

Frank looked down at the pad and tried to decipher the scribbles. "Hermione, looks like?"

"That's it. Hermione Marsh."

Frank thanked the officer and stepped out into the hall and turned left. By now a few neighbors had returned home and were furtively peeking out of their doors at the commotion. Some of the doors closed quickly as Frank strode purposefully down the hall. He knocked on 1207.

The door was answered by a bright-eyed lady who identified herself as Hermione Marsh and invited Frank in, once he had shown his ID. She looked as if she were still shaken up by her discovery of Doctor Hesterberg's body.

"So tell me exactly what happened?" Frank began. He had not been asked if he wanted to sit, and to be honest, he didn't.

"Well, I was coming home from work. I'm a bookkeeper and I got off early. I was coming down the hallway from the elevator and I happened to notice that Maurice—I mean Professor Hesterberg's— door was slightly ajar. I often say hello to him when we run into one another, so I just sort of called out as I went by. Of course there was no answer. Then I saw the foot in the doorway. I stopped and peeked in and...that's when I saw there was a body."

"Did you open the door?"

She shook her head up and down vigorously, as if to shake the memory out of her head. "Yes, I'm afraid I did. I saw him lying there."

"What did you do next?"

"I turned and ran for my apartment. I panicked. It was horrible. It didn't even occur to me he might not be dead. He looked dead."

"Do you remember hearing or seeing anything else? Any indication there might have been someone else in the apartment?"

"I don't remember anything. As I said, I was shocked. All that occurred to me was to run, to get safe in my own place."

"And you called the police immediately?"

"Well…I probably took a few minutes to calm myself down."

Frank had already noticed a bit of the aroma of gin on Hermione's breath. "Maybe you took a few deep breaths, had a drink to relax yourself, things like that?"

"Yes, that's exactly what I did, in fact. After a few short minutes I was in possession of my faculties again, and I telephoned the police. It couldn't have been more than five minutes or so."

Frank's ever-present notebook was open and he was jotting rapidly as he spoke. "Did you leave your apartment again after that at all, perhaps to take another look, find someone else to tell about it, anything like that?"

"No, I've been in here ever since. To tell you the truth I'm still spooked about going out in that hall again."

"Did you perhaps call another neighbor, the building manager or superintendent, anyone like that?"

"There is no building superintendent. There are maintenance people that come during the day but try to find one. Everybody on our floor works and wouldn't be home yet—everyone but Professor Hesterberg, that is. He's often home during the week. Oh dear. I mean, he *was* often home. This is so awful."

"Perhaps you called a friend to decompress, tell them what happened?"

"Yes, in fact. I called my friends Renée and Simon. I talked about it with Renée for a while and she helped me calm down. She said I had done exactly the right thing and should just stay in here tonight, have a drink and read or watch television, and that's what I plan to do."

"And you didn't see or hear anything else that comes to mind, anything at all?"

She thought for a long time before shaking her head. "No, I can't recall a thing, Detective."

"All right, thank you, Miss? Mrs.?"

"It's Miss, I suppose. Divorced, though I decided to keep his last name. Didn't get much else of his to keep when all was said and done. Most people call me Hermione. Feel free to call me Hermione if you're comfortable."

She gave him a bit of a mischievous smile. Marlon might have liked her, Frank reflected.

"Thank you, Miss Marsh, here's my card in case you think of anything else that might be of help. I think your plan to stay in tonight is a good one."

He scanned the room quickly and his eyes lit on a table by the couch that faced a wide screen television. The blue-cast gin bottle was resting on the table next to a glass and a silver bucket of ice. It was hard to tell how far down the level, but he figured Hermione was set for the evening. He wondered if she'd be watching Gaslight on the classic movie channel.

* * * *

He returned to the crime scene and carefully walked around, staying out of the way of the techs at work but trying to absorb whatever information he could. He compared his memories of being here two days previously, replayed his conversation with Hesterberg, looked around for something, anything, that might afford an insight. Had anything been moved? Was anything clearly disturbed?

He asked the techs a few questions. It appeared from the evidence that the assailant had not entered further into the room, had touched very little, if anything. They were dusting for prints on the doorbell and the door. It was conceivable the attacker had avoided touching much of anything. Had he (or she) rung the bell, or knocked?

There was a peephole in the door. Logic dictated Hesterberg wouldn't have just opened the door to anybody; it likely was someone he recognized and knew. Maybe even was expecting.

Frank looked around for the phone. It was resting on the kitchen counter. Was there a pad? Perhaps he had written something down? No, nothing to be found. No notes, not even on the refrigerator. Nothing written anywhere.

Just that crazy note. IT'S HER FAULT.

What did that mean? Was it Margo?

Well, if Hesterberg had been surprised at the door by his wife and she had killed him right there and then, he wouldn't exactly have had time to sit down at his computer and print out a note like that and bring it back with him.

He asked the techs if someone could find and inspect Hesterberg's computer and printer, see if there was any record of having created a word-processing file or printed it, and fingerprint the keyboard.

There was a study/den where Hesterberg worked, and they located the electronics there, along with another phone (no note pads there either) and went to work on them. It was a long shot but he was grasping at straws here. Likely the assailant had not entered the room so would not have gone to the computer and printed out the note. Either he or she had brought it with them with the specific idea of leaving it behind, or Hesterberg already had created it and had it in his possession at the moment he opened the door and was killed.

He walked around further, slowly checking every room. Was anything standing out to him?

His phone buzzed. It was Monica. He snapped it open.

"Detective? You called me?"

"Did you locate Margo? Was she in her apartment?"

"No. I went over there tonight; the super went in with me. We looked all over. No sign of her."

"Did it look as if she had packed or taken anything?"

"I didn't really look. Why?"

"Is there anywhere you can think of that she might go? I need to locate her as soon as I can."

"Has something happened?"

"I can't talk about that right this moment. What I need to know is some way I can find Margo."

"I can't think of anything."

"Can you do me a favor, and call her super back, tell her I'm coming over and will need to get into her apartment? Just to let her know, save a few minutes. Tell her not to go into the apartment herself, just to expect me shortly."

"Well, sure. But what's going on? Is Max making more threats?"

"As I said, I can't tell you anything just yet. Thanks for helping me out."

He snapped the phone shut and took one last look around the scene. There was nothing else he could think of just yet. The apartment would be sealed off for at least a few days. He could come back fresh tomorrow when he might have more concrete evidence to work with. He headed out to the elevator. The techs had already fingerprinted it and no doubt had done some fingerprinting in the lobby, but he knew those were long shots. How many people passed through that lobby and this elevator every day? Still, he admired the thoroughness of the SID's crew.

* * * *

Judy, the Super Lady, was waiting to buzz him in as soon as he hit the front door. He didn't even have to go down the stairs; she was in the lobby by the time he had come through both sets of glass entry doors, looking apprehensive.

"What's up, Detective?" she asked.

"If you can let me in to Margo Hesterberg's apartment it would be greatly appreciated," he said brusquely.

"Glad to see you too. Sure, follow me."

She turned around and headed back down the hall to the rear of the building, twirling the key on her ring in one hand as she walked.

Frank wasn't quite sure what he expected to find but he knew the first thing he wanted to look for. It was a small apartment; finding the bedroom was not a challenge. He donned a new pair of disposable gloves and opened the closet door. The tiny closet smelled of some kind of sachet. There were a few empty hangers on the rod.

He turned to the bureau and pulled open the top drawer, which held underwear, socks, and other small items. There were spaces. The second drawer was mostly shirts, and again he saw uneven piles.

"Would you say Margo Hesterberg is a careful woman?" he asked as he perused the contents of the drawers in rapid order.

"Um, what exactly do you mean?"

"Would you say she's a *neat* woman? This apartment looks very well kept, everything in its place. No clutter."

"Don't know her all that well, but yeah, I'd say she's a bit *fastidious*," Judy replied, punching the word sarcastically. "Not that I come in here all that often, but let me tell you, if this were my place and my hubby weren't around, I'd probably have a bit more of a mess, you know?"

"Not the kind of person who'd make uneven piles in her drawers like these," Frank said, more to himself than to her. "She's packed recently, and in a hurry."

He looked around the closet again. There was a shelf above the clothes rod, with a few boxes stored away. There was an open space at the top. Maybe that was how Margo had arranged it, but Frank's hunch was that there had been a suitcase of some kind up there.

"What was the last time you saw Margo Hesterberg?" he asked.

She thought for a moment. "Let me see...a few days ago? Yeah, ran into her coming off the elevator the other day."

"She was coming off the elevator? She lives on the ground floor!"

"No no...I was coming off the elevator. Coming down from a tenant upstairs. She was in the basement near my apartment, in the laundry."

"She was doing her laundry? What day was that?"

Judy's lips moved as she thought hard about it, counting. "Four days ago. No, five. It was Saturday. Five days ago."

"Did you talk about anything? Did she say anything about planning to do anything or go anywhere?"

Judy shrugged. "Naw, nothing like that. We just said hi, ships passing in the night. I'm not that involved or friendly with any of my tenants."

"She had laundry with her?"

"I'm not sure, but she was coming out of the laundry room. That's the last time I saw her."

"Your husband is superintendent with you too, right? Would he possibly have encountered her at some later time?"

"Well, let's go ask him," Judy said. "When you're done here."

"Could you maybe call him and ask him to come up here?"

Judy sighed. "Yeah, sure. I'll go get him. You seem trustworthy enough up here."

"Actually I'd prefer you stay, can you call him?"

Frank knew protocol well enough to play it safe. He was already on shaky ground, having gained entry to this apartment without a warrant or due cause. Likely whatever he might uncover here was useless as evidence in a court of law if it ever came to that. But he had no idea where this line of inquiry was heading; accusations of falsifying or contaminating evidence would be another matter altogether. If they later found it necessary to return with a bona fide warrant, he wanted to do his best to sidestep questions about things like planted evidence, so he needed to *not* be left alone here for even a moment.

He was fortunate Judy was being so obliging in any case, but then she still was laboring under the misapprehension that he was here because Margo might be in danger. She gave off another mighty sigh, rolled her eyes skyward, and pulled her phone from her pocket.

Frank continued to move about the apartment, looking for any other signs that might tell him where Margo could have gone. Again he checked for pads by the phone, without luck. He looked for a computer and found an aging one on a stand in her bedroom, but he couldn't do much more than power it up. He couldn't access anything without a password.

Judy's husband, a burly balding man in a white tee shirt who introduced himself as Steve, arrived in the apartment. Frank asked a few quick questions and established that Steve had not encountered "Miz Hesterberg" any time since his wife had. He left another card with them both and asked that they contact him if they remembered or learned anything that might help him locate her.

It was getting late but he needed to put things together while the trail might still be warm. Heading back to his car, he struggled to find some sense in what had happened.

Max Hesterberg insists Margo is trying to kill him, but has nothing definite to back it up, just "feelings."

Margo, who has made similar claims to her sister that Hesterberg threatened *her*, disappears.

Hesterberg turns up dead.

Margo apparently has moved out, to parts unknown, with whatever a suitcase will hold.

She likely hasn't gone far.

Frank pulled out his phone to call Monica. He apologized for bothering her again but said he needed to speak with her one more time. Yes, right now.

* * * *

"So you're telling me Max is dead?" Monica was having a hard time making sense of it all. They were once again sitting in her parlor. Frank was once again jotting in his notebook. "Murdered? You think Margo murdered him?"

"I don't know who murdered him, but yes, he was killed today. Your sister is certainly a suspect. Once again I have to ask you to think carefully. Is there anywhere Margo might have gone, anything you can tell me that might help me find her?"

Monica's eyes were wide and looking glazed. She just kept shaking her head. "She couldn't have done this. It makes no sense."

Frank repeated his question. This time she seemed to snap back to reality and she looked at him, continuing to shake her head.

"No, I've got no idea where she could be. She didn't do this, Detective."

"All the more reason I need to find her right away. If she's innocent, she needs to make me see it."

He was getting nowhere. He stood up and packed away his notebook.

"You've got my card. Please, call me any time night or day if you come up with anything, if you hear from her, anything that would help. If she's innocent I can help her, but I've got to find her, do you understand?"

Monica also rose, nodding her head gravely.

"One last thing: do you have a recent photo of her that I can borrow?" He realized he had never seen Margo Hesterberg.

"Yes, of course." Frank expected her to run for a photo album or a framed picture on a wall or a mantle. Instead she reached for a cell phone on a nearby table and began pressing buttons. She held up her phone to show a picture of her and her sister smiling at an outdoor cafe. Margo looked very much like her sister only a bit more youthful, her hair and face a little fuller, with a more animated and buoyant expression.

No more framed snapshots. Frank again felt like a dinosaur as he looked at the phone screen.

"Can you email that to me?" he sighed. He reached back into his pocket for his pencil so he could write his address for her.

"Certainly. But why write it? Don't you have it on your phone so you can just send it to me?"

He thought of his Neanderthal flip phone. "No, Ms. Wersching, I'm afraid my phone doesn't do that. But my email address is easy enough." He looked about for something on which to write. Monica smiled in spite of her state of mind.

"Just tell it to me," she said. "I'll send you a picture right now." She hit more buttons as he rattled it off and then pressed SEND. There was a "bwwwoop" sound and she said, "Done."

Oh brave new world, thought Frank. He figured Doctor Max would have approved that he knew the line. He might have said, "So you're a reader, then..."

He stopped back at the station before calling it a night. The night shift had taken over and it was fairly quiet, which he welcomed. He sat at his desk, flipping through his notes, trying to organize everything and find a pattern. He reconstructed Hesterberg's condo in his mind's eye, the crime scene...then Margo's apartment, looking for something to jump out and announce itself. Years of experience had taught him that this was often fruitful, but there was nothing. Nothing yet.

The photo of Margo, he discovered, was indeed waiting for him on his computer. He clicked the onscreen button to print out several copies.

As he waited for the printer, he started scribbling his course of action onto a legal pad with a ballpoint pen.

First order of business: find Margo Hesterberg. Underlined twice.

Second order of business: find out anybody else who might fit the role as the murderer. That is to say: being known to Hesterberg sufficiently for him to open the door to them while also having motive to harm him.

Next destination, check the university.

He jotted a few more thoughts down, then walked over to the shared printer and picked up the copies of Margo's picture.

There was one last thing he could do tonight, for what it was worth. He returned to his computer and sent out emails in his established routes throughout the department, with the attached photo, requesting an alert on Margo Hesterberg.

In the morning he could follow up on that with more alerts and requests for BOLOs—Be On the Lookout notices—through various channels.

He yawned. Nothing else he could do tonight unless Monica called. Something else experience had taught him was that even while he slept his mind would keep working, looking for connections. There had been times when he had awakened in the morning with an insight bouncing around his head that hadn't been in there the night before.

Might as well call it a night.

THREE

The night had not provided new insight, Frank had to admit. But then again it hadn't provided much sleep, either. He had found himself awake several times, his brain racing in overdrive. He was awake when his alarm went off.

He wondered if guilt wasn't a component of that. Could he have taken more seriously the concerns of Maurice Hesterberg and perhaps prevented his killing? Second guessing came with the job, he knew by now, and it was best to try to put those kinds of thoughts out of mind as best he could. Get the feet on the ground before the head can completely kick in. Shave, shower, coffee, breakfast, get in the car, drive to work, all by the numbers. Do not listen to the head until absolutely necessary.

His yellow legal pad, with his notes of the evening before, was still on his desk to greet him when he arrived at the squad room.

Things were already bustling around him, detectives and officers scurrying about and talking loudly, everybody multi-tasking to try to get that much more done already. The city was always generously dropping something new on the detectives' doorstep, and it was always a challenge to stay on top of it all.

He loved the oddness of the name of his unit, Personal Crimes. Some years back it had been called Special Crimes and before that plain old Robbery-Homicide, but at some point a commission decided Personal Crimes had a more meaningful ring to it, the sound of a true mission statement. They still dealt with basically the same types of felony offenses: murders, severe assaults, serious robberies.

The unit, one flight up, that handled burglaries and similar non-violent crimes had been re-named Property Crimes, which to his thinking was somewhat more lackluster. Frank had to wonder who would ever want to transfer to something called Property Crimes.

He turned on his computer, gave his prior night's notes a once-over, and began to map out his day. Getting out an official BOLO on Margo was his priority, along with whatever else he could do to get the word out on her. Next he would head to the university to try to find close associates of Hesterberg.

His thoughts were interrupted by the buzzy ringtone of his cell phone. He fished it out of his pocket. "Vandegraf."

"Yeah, Frank, this is Coulton, up here in Sunnyview. I got your email alert this morning first thing."

Sunnyview was the northernmost district of the city, and formed part of the boundary with its neighbor city. It was mostly suburban, with malls, restaurants, hotels, and the like. Sam Coulton was a detective and worked the northern division. He was a righteous cop in Frank's eyes, unsentimental to the point of cynicism and not exactly lovable, but righteous nonetheless. Frank always included him in his notices and inquiries and had often been rewarded for doing so.

"Yeah, Sam, what's up?"

"I've found your girl."

"My girl? Margo Hesterberg?"

"The same."

"Where are you?" Frank realized he had begun to rise out of his seat. He sat back down, grabbed his pen and pulled his pad over to jot down the address.

"I'm at the Pleasant Dreams Inn, the one up near the Expressway. You know it?"

Pleasant Dreams was a regional chain, on the inexpensive side of things but famously clean and family friendly.

"Oh yeah. Where exactly?"

"Room 816. All the way in the back, past the pool."

"Don't know how you found her, but this is great. Hang on to her, I'll be right over."

"Well, that's the thing," sighed Sam. "She's not going anywhere. You can take your time."

* * * *

There were several city vans in the parking lot, from the coroner and the Scientific Investigation Division. Frank worked his way through the uniformed officers who were doing their best to wrangle the herd of curious and excited people who had gathered there, just outside of the building.

He attached his badge to his lanyard and hung it around his neck to facilitate the task of continually displaying it to still another beleaguered uniform. It was a short walk down the hallway to room 816, where the usual clump of techs and medical examiners were at work.

Sam himself was standing in the room, hands in pockets, talking with a tech. They were next to a queen-size bed upon which lay a body that had been covered with a sheet for the moment. Sam saw Frank and nodded in acknowledgment, then motioned him over. He lifted the sheet off the head of the body.

It was indeed Margo Hesterberg, or at least she was a dead ringer for her picture. She was on her back, arms at her sides, eyes starkly open and staring at the ceiling.

Frank could see the ligature marks on her bare throat.

"This your girl?" Sam asked brightly.

"Sure looks like her," Frank said, rubbing the back of his neck.

"You still do that," Sam remarked, pointing to Frank's hand on his neck.

What, now he was famous for it? Self-consciously, he dropped his hand to his side.

"There was ID?" Frank asked.

"Yeah, her bag was on that chair over there. Margo Hesterberg she is."

"What happened?"

"Housekeeper found her this morning. Funny thing, you know those signs you can put on your door, one side says DO NOT DIS-TURB and the other says MAID SERVICE REQUESTED? Well, the sign requesting service was on the doorknob, so she unlocked the door and came in. There she was."

"What time was this?" Frank asked, starting to look about the room.

"Early. Maybe seven thirty? Best guess is she was murdered yes-terday, maybe last night. We got here right about the time I called you this morning. I was first up and got the call."

"Has she been touched or processed in any way?"

"Not yet. When you said you were on the way over, and the MEs showed up, I told 'em to wait for you."

Sam pointed alongside Margo's body on the still-made bed. "Looks like she's been strangled. That the murder weapon, you think?"

A long beige fabric cord, something like one would use to pull open curtains or drapes, lay next to her.

"If so, they bothered to remove the cord from her throat after she was dead," Frank observed. "It's like they took their time."

"There's also this," Sam continued, pointing to something peeking out from under the sheet that had been laid over her. Sam reached out and swiped away the sheet without touching what was beneath. It brought to mind the old magician's trick, swiping a tablecloth out from under a fully set dinner table without disturbing a plate or the candelabra. Frank almost expected him to exclaim, "Ta-daa!"

There was a piece of light cardboard, perhaps five inches square, lying alongside her body. On it had been printed, with a broad-tip black marker in large block letters, three words:

IT'S HIS FAULT

Frank had already donned his gloves and now he bent over the body, careful not to come into contact with it, and gingerly picked up the cardboard by the smallest edge of a corner. He turned it over, looked at it for a long time. There was nothing else written on the card anywhere, no marks or smudges. It was immaculate. Even the printing was neat and precise.

"What in...?" Frank began.

"Pretty cryptic, I'd say," Sam offered. "Who's *he*?"

"You don't know the half of it," Frank muttered.

He replaced the card where he had found it. Now he leaned back over the body carefully in order to inspect it. She was fully clothed in a blue long-sleeved shirt and denim slacks, short white socks and a pair of tennis shoes.

Frank delicately picked up each hand and inspected it. Her fingernails were unpolished and clipped very short. Likely she had struggled—strangulation is a most unpleasant way to die—but the odds were reduced of their finding any skin cells under the nails.

"Looks to me like she was taken by surprise," Sam observed. "Not a huge fight out of her."

Frank inspected the head and face. "No bruising that I can see. Doesn't look like she was knocked unconscious first or anything."

He motioned to the medical examiner in charge who came closer.

"You can go ahead," Frank said. "Just make sure the techs get pictures first, okay?"

The ME nodded wearily. Apparently he was at the end of his shift rather than the beginning. He waggled a finger at a couple of the techs and passed the word. The moment they approached, Frank pointed out the card and made sure they knew to photograph it profusely, print it, and bag it for further processing as evidence. He also made sure they photographed and bagged the cord.

Frank watched as they turned the body over and began their examination. Of course there would be a much more thorough one once the body had been transferred to the coroner's office, but whatever he could glean right now would possibly be of great importance.

"Time of death?" he asked at one point. The examiner gave him a frame of sometime between five and eight the previous night.

Margo was still alive when Max had been killed.

With all due respect to the dead, she hadn't been cleared yet.

His own inspection of the motel room didn't yield any insights. There seemed to be no sign of forced entry. Officers had canvassed the floor and nobody in any of the nearby rooms could remember having heard any noises of an argument, a struggle, or an assault. The manager had pointed out that at midweek like this, occupancy was lower, and the few guests here were possibly out to dinner or elsewhere.

There were no obvious signs of forced entry into the room or any kind of violent struggle or confrontation. The assailant had apparently gained entry without much problem, had surprised Margo and overcome her easily. Had she simply let him or her into the room?

Her handbag yielded nothing unusual. There was a wallet, keys, the other typical things one would expect. Frank found nothing particularly worthy of attention. It would all be collected and recorded and he could look through it later. He did take the car keys, making sure to inform the techs that he would be returning them shortly.

Margo's small suitcase sat closed on the usual luggage stand found in these kinds of rooms. She hadn't bothered to put anything in any of the drawers. A blouse and a jacket looked lonely hanging in the otherwise empty closet. Her hotel key card sat on the nightstand next to the bed.

According to desk records, she had checked in Tuesday, three days ago, using her real name. She had used a credit card to reserve the room through the coming weekend. Frank made a note to stop by the desk and see who had checked her in.

Sam broke his reverie. "I assume this one's yours now." He looked downright relieved.

Frank nodded, twisting his mouth into a grimace. He didn't want it, but it had to be his.

Among other things, that meant it fell to him to inform Monica Wersching about her sister's fate. That would have to be his next stop.

He finished his inspection, consulted with the techs, made a few more requests. He knew most of the crew and for the most part felt he could rely on their expertise and thoroughness. Then he headed off to the front desk. The officers outside had already dispersed a fair amount of the crowd and he easily traversed the parking lot to the lobby.

He at least lucked out in that the clerk who had checked in Margo was on duty. He was a neat and nervous young man, perhaps in his late twenties, evidently seriously shaken by the death of Margo Hesterberg. He vaguely recalled her arrival and dug out the sign-in record. She was alone. She had left a credit card number as a deposit until check out, along with her real name and home address and her car's license plate number. The clerk explained that the hotel required that every guest display a parking pass in their car's front window while in the lot, and this was checked regularly. There was a description of Margo's car.

Frank recorded everything in his notebook. The clerk wasn't much help beyond that. His memory corresponded with what the uniforms had learned: she had checked in on Tuesday and booked the room for seven days in total. She had made no small talk that the clerk could remember, and he had not seen her since. Frank asked for the manager and ascertained that nobody currently on duty had had any contact with Margo in the past two days. The night shift would be coming on in a few hours and the manager would also ask them the same question; Frank was welcome to check back with him again.

Frank wandered out into the parking lot and began looking for Margo's small gold Honda Fit. It wasn't difficult to locate. He tried Margo's key alarm and heard the low beep and click that indicated he had unlocked the door. It was a fastidiously-kept car (Judy the super had characterized Margo correctly, it seemed): clean, free of any loose refuse, and even with a slight scent of floral air freshener. Her parking pass was displayed on the dash in the window. Only a small square box of tissues rested on the passenger seat. He checked the box and found nothing else stuck into it—just tissues. There was very little in the glove box besides the vehicle registration, nothing in any of the other little nooks and crannies that newer cars seemed to feature. He checked under the seats and opened the hatchback to look into the rear storage area. The car seemed almost empty.

If Margo had indeed murdered Max, she hadn't brought the murder weapon here with her.

When he was convinced he wasn't going to find anything, he locked the car and trudged back to Room 816 to return the key and tell the techs where they would find the Honda. There was nothing more he could do here. He would have to wait on the techs for further information. He thanked Sam for getting in touch with him and departed.

His next task was one he did not relish. He pulled out his phone to call Monica Wersching and say he was on his way over.

Not surprisingly, Monica did not take the news well but, all things considered, Frank thought she took it better than he had anticipated. She had invited him in with visible apprehension, they had sat down in her parlor, and she had broken into tears before he had even finished his first sentence.

Over the years this unpleasant duty had fallen to Frank way too many times, and it never got any easier or less awkward. He had become inured to gruesome crime scenes and grisly modes of death, but had never hardened to breaking the heart of a loved one.

He waited it out in respectful silence. She regained her composure after a few minutes, wiped her eyes, and steadied her voice to ask him for further details of Margo's death. He kept it as simple as he could.

One of her first comments was, "So there's no possible way that Max killed her."

"No, her death definitely occurred after his. I'm sorry, I know this is hard, but can you think of anyone else who might have had reason to do this?"

"My God, no." She shook her head repeatedly, staring down at her hands. "Margo was a sweetheart."

"Let's go back to those break-ins Margo believed were occurring in her apartment. Could that have been done by someone other than Max?"

"I don't know who."

"Was there anybody who had a key to her place?"

"I didn't even have one, and I was the closest person to her."

"If she were to go away, did she ever have, I don't know, plants that needed watering? A cat or some pet needing to be fed?"

"No pets. Margo might have had plants but she never went away so she never asked me to come water them. It's possible lately she was so agitated that I think she just got rid of them or let them die."

"So there's nobody she might have asked to look in on her place at any point."

"The only people who might have had a key to her place were the supers. The property managers." She thought for a minute and then hastily added, "I can't believe they would have done anything to hurt her."

"And there's nobody you can think of that she'd been in touch with recently, nobody you saw her with, nobody she might have mentioned?"

Monica gave that some thought. It was clear she was having trouble concentrating at the moment. "No. I can't think of anyone she had been in touch with besides Max. As I told you before, she kept her own counsel in recent times."

Frank tried a few more questions but nothing seemed promising. From experience he realized there was only so far he could go at this point, so he thanked Monica and said he would be in touch and asked her to call with anything she might think would be helpful.

"I suppose I'll need to go organize Margo's things," Monica said rather distractedly as Frank rose from his seat.

"Maybe it would be better to wait on that," Frank said. "Let me talk to the supers first. Give it a couple of days, okay?"

Monica just nodded. Thinking on his last trip to the apartment, somehow he didn't think it would yield anything all that promising, but what else was there?

At the building entry, he rang the intercom for Steve and Judy's apartment but didn't have to wait to be buzzed in because a young man pulled the door open and slipped by him, followed by Judy herself.

"Detective," she greeted him dryly. "We must stop meeting like this. My husband is starting to get suspicious."

"I'm afraid I'm going to need to get into Margo Hesterberg's apartment again."

She rolled her eyes. "I don't think she's come back, and I'm guessing you haven't found her yet, huh?"

"Actually, I have, but let me tell you inside."

Now she looked alarmed. "Something happen to her?"

"Just let me in, okay ?"

Judy yelled out to the young man, who had stopped and turned to wait for her. "Emil, I'll be along in a few minutes, you know what to do with the trash, right?" He nodded and resumed walking out to the street.

"Pickup day tomorrow morning, we have to roll the garbage bins out to the street for the trucks. Come on, I'll get the key." He followed her to the elevator.

"Your son?" asked Frank.

"Emil? Oh, no. We've got a grown son but he lives in another state. Emil just does work for us, like when we need a strong back or an extra pair of hands. Good guy."

A quick stop at her apartment for the key then back upstairs, and they were at the door. Frank stopped her before they entered. She looked at him apprehensively. "Is she all right?"

"No, I'm afraid not. Judy, Margo Hesterberg is dead. We found her body this morning."

That stopped her cold in her tracks. She just stared at Frank for a moment, her mouth agape.

"Wh-what happened?" she stammered.

"She was murdered."

Frank's long silence finally got through to her that he was not going to be forthcoming about details. She fumbled the key into the lock and opened the door. Frank had already pulled out a pair of his disposable gloves and was donning them.

"I'm going to have to ask you to not touch anything this time." He stepped into the apartment, looking around.

"I've been in here now and then," Judy said, "including with you. I've touched plenty. My prints are all around."

"I'm not worried about your prints so much as I am of something more recent being covered up," Frank said. "I understand someone had been breaking into this apartment and moving things around,. Did Margo ever mention that to you?"

"Uh, yeah, sure. She wanted the locks changed. We did that for her about two weeks ago."

"What exactly did she tell you had been happening?"

"She said she came home one evening to find a vase broken, just smashed to pieces on her hall floor. She told me it had been in another room."

"And there was no cat or dog to knock it over, right?"

"No, Margo has no pets. I mean, *had* no pets. We discourage them. Anyway, she claimed the vase had to have been carried from the other room and brought into the hallway. She said a few other things had happened...she called them 'subtle' things. Items moved from one place to another."

"Did she specify any of those?"

Judy thought about it, hands on hips. "I kinda didn't pay a lot of attention. Steve thinks she's a little ditsy and she was being paranoid. He thinks she just forgot she had moved the...yes, that was one! She said a group of old photos had been taken out of her dresser drawer and spread out on her bed one night!" She paused to think some more. "There was something about something from college. A transcript, I think she might have said, a yearbook, something like that, that were stored in her closet and she found them on her night table. I don't remember much more than that."

"That was pretty good, actually."

"Well, Steve made a kind of joke about it, saying she was reliving her past, pulling out old memories, and then just forgot. That's why it might have stuck in my mind."

Frank was carefully looking around the entry hall, bending down to check the carpet and floor, inspecting the small photographs on the wall, slowly working his way to the living room. Even with his gloves he was trying to touch as little as possible. He intended on having the techs in here as soon as he could.

"From just where was Margo returning when she would find these things? I understand she didn't go out much."

"Pretty much always from visiting her sister, I think. She and I weren't exactly friendly, you know? We don't get real friendly with the tenants, it can cause complications. But the impression I got was that she stayed home a lot, kept to herself."

"And how did you get that impression exactly?"

Super Judy might have been getting a bit unnerved by Frank as he asked questions while seemingly paying all his attention to the apartment.

She shifted the weight back and forth on her feet. "Well, I never saw any visitors, except her sister. I seldom ran into her around the building. Steve once or twice remarked the same thing. We do keep our eyes open for strangers around here."

Somehow Frank suspected that Steve and Judy knew considerably more about some of their tenants than they would have let on. He had known a few nosy, gossipy type property managers in his day. What had tipped her off, she seemed to be saying, was that she did *not* know anything about anyone visiting Margo.

He was in the living room now, beginning to methodically make his away around the room. He raised a hand to Judy. "Please, I'd appreciate it if you stay in the hall for now. Who has a key to this apartment?"

"What exactly do you mean?"

"Well, of course Margo had one. More than one?"

"She got one set from us, for the front door, the apartment, and the outdoor garbage bin area. Naturally she could have duplicated them, tenants usually do, but we gave her one set."

"And of course *you* have a key to this apartment."

Judy raised her hands as if to say, "Well, here we are, aren't we?" and remained silent, giving Frank a wide-eyed look.

"Anybody else to your knowledge?"

"Not that I know of. If the management company or anybody like that visits, they have to come to us."

Frank nodded, bending over to look under an old low sofa. "And you and Steve keep a close watch on your sets of keys, I'm sure?"

"We certainly do. You saw, they're kept in a closet, and we lock it if we're not going to be around for any reason."

He reached under the sofa and gingerly picked something up between thumb and forefinger. He brought it out and looked at it closely. It seemed to be little shard of glass or ceramic.

"Do you know what the vase that was broken looked like?"

"Search me. She swept it up and threw it away. Nobody ever came in here to clean."

Frank put the little shard back where he had found it. "She kept this place pretty clean by herself. No housekeeper or cleaning lady or anything, then?"

"Not that I know of. And I usually see them when they come in here. As I said, we're on the lookout for unfamiliar types in the building. We ask tenants to inform us if they are going to have regular visitors like cleaners. You know, so when we see them we know they're supposed to be here, they're not suspicious."

Frank had resumed his slow steady perusal of the room. "Seen anybody like that around here in the past few weeks?"

"Suspicious sorts?" Again she paused to consider. "No, not really. Nobody."

"What does 'not really' mean, exactly?"

"Well, sure there have been people coming and going in the building all the time. But nobody we couldn't *account* for, you know? Delivery people, plumber, legitimate visitors, that kind of stuff."

"You'd know if someone was 'not accounted for,' then?"

"We keep an eye out, yes."

"And nobody like that came to Margo's door to your knowledge? Package delivery, repairman, anything like that?"

"Repair and maintenance, we have to call for, and no, nobody like that. No deliveries that I know. People have to ring to get in and that generally means I'm aware of them."

Frank continued through the apartment, asking Judy to remain in the hallway until he arrived in the bedroom.

"Do you happen to know where she found the photographs or the yearbook or whatever it was? Or where they came from?" he called out.

"I never saw any of it," she called back. "She said the stuff came from her dresser and her closet, so I guess it was all in there. She said some of it was laid out across her bed and some of it across her living room table."

He checked the cardboard boxes he had seen earlier in the closet. He carefully pulled each one down and checked it. One did indeed hold a pile of college memorabilia: yearbooks, a diploma, transcripts, even a few old essays and papers.

At the very top of one box was a typical college term paper with a cover page bearing her name, a note scrawled in red across the top. Frank labored his way through the writing: "Nicely done, very nicely done, but then I shall always expect nice things from you. Max." The date was twenty-six years ago.

Max had begun to court his student, and it seemed he wasn't very discreet about it either.

A pile of photos filled another box. They weren't stacked as neatly as most of her other things. Possibly, he surmised, these were the pictures she found spread out across her bed, and she had hurriedly repacked them and stuffed them up into the closet. They were photos from her school days or thereabouts. Most of them featured a girl who looked a lot like the picture he had of Margo, only younger and more jubilant. He didn't recognize anybody else in the pictures except for Max—a younger thinner Max with more hair, including resplendent sideburns and a goatee.

He returned the photos to the box and left it alongside the others out on the floor..

He proceeded in similar fashion for another half hour, then paused and called in a request for a processing team from the SID, making special note of the boxes he had laid out in the bedroom. It was all a long shot that any prints or other evidence could be pulled off this material, but he had to give it a shot.

He checked the back door. There were two strong locks on it. No noticeable scratches or marks around the hardware to suggest forced entry. The door had glass panes but they were solid, no digs or gouges in the wood.

Finally he returned to the entryway. "Margo never reported any break-in from the back yard, did she?"

Judy was beginning to look bored. "Never. But she did have us install that second lock on the door."

"There will be a crime scene investigation team coming here. I'm going to ask you to stay out of here before they arrive, and to direct them here and let them in."

"Sure. I'll be happy to stay out. This is starting to give me the creeps already."

As Judy locked the door behind them, Frank said, "I have to go to my car to get something. Can you let me back in in just a second?"

He returned with a roll of yellow police tape reading DO NOT CROSS and a roll of adhesive, and affixed a criss-cross across the front of the jamb that did not touch the door itself. The techs would remove it when they arrived, but hopefully it would keep out anybody else who was curious.

"I told you, I'm not going in there," Judy said.

"It's not for you," Frank replied.

Neither one totally bought that, he reflected. But she simply nodded and said, "Okay. Anyway, I gotta go help Emil move those bins. Until next time, Detective."

FOUR

It wasn't really that late, it was just feeling that way already. His next stop was the State University, which seemed a logical step in trying to track down information about Max Hesterberg.

He decided he'd start with the administration offices, out of courtesy, and work his way down to the English Department and some of Max's colleagues.

The first person to meet with him was Dean Marian Wormley, a lean, dignified woman with a well-styled mane of silvery hair. She greeted Frank in the reception area with a look of deep sadness.

"Detective, we've all heard the news about dear Doctor Hesterberg and we are all devastated. What a horrible thing." She motioned to a large maroon velvet upholstered sofa and they both sat down.

"Yes, ma'am," Frank replied seriously.

"'Dean' is fine," she corrected. "'Dean Wormley' is my correct title." She looked at him expectantly.

"Of course, uh, Dean Wormley. It was a terrible tragedy. My condolences to you and everyone at the University."

Titles seemed to be extremely important to academic types, he considered.

"So how may I be of help, Detective?"

"I would like to speak with anyone who knew Doctor Hesterberg well. I have a lot of questions. You're a logical place to begin. Did you know him well?"

"I must admit, I hardly knew the man at all. We spoke at a few gatherings and social events here. He seemed a nice enough man— struck me as quite self-confident, perhaps to the point of being a bit supercilious. Competent enough from what I saw of his faculty records. He published some well received papers in his area of expertise."

"Were there ever any disagreements, controversies, involving you?"

She frowned then raised her eyebrows. "No. Nothing like that."

She just gazed quietly at him waiting for his next question. The conversation continued with more abrupt answers and awkward silences. Frank could see it was going nowhere. He thanked her for her time and asked if he might be directed to somebody closer to Hesterberg.

She stood up, shook his hand briskly while looking him in the eye, and said, "Let me know if I might be of any further help to you, Detective Vanderwaal. We all hope you get to the bottom of this."

"That's Vandegraf," Frank corrected. "Thank you, Dean Wormley."

The chairman of the English Department seemed more promising. Mark Wootten said he had known Max Hesterberg for over thirty years and counted him as a valued friend as well as an esteemed colleague. In fact, Wootten had counted himself among that suspect Cognac-quaffing group known to Margo Hesterberg as Max's "tavern companions."

It was evident that he was sorely shaken by the death of his friend and wanted to help however he could. Frank remarked that Dean Wormley had recommended that he begin his inquiry with Wootten.

At the mention of Wormley, Wootten screwed up his face into a sour scowl. "So you've met the Wicked Witch of the West. Quite a piece of work, that one."

"She says that she and Hesterberg were not well acquainted."

"She told you that! Fascinating. Did she mention the knock-down drag-out battles at the budget meetings?"

"Uh, no."

"Interesting. She must have known it would come out."

"She and Hesterberg had words?"

"Numerous times. Marian is used to having her way. Max was one to speak his mind. They were the proverbial oil and water. Or perhaps I should say he was gasoline to her bonfire. Or perhaps…"

Frank jumped in to short circuit the search for additional metaphors. "What did they argue about?"

Wootten waved a hand in dismissal. "Oh, nothing of import. It was the principle of the thing. Max didn't like her and didn't want her to have her way, so he made himself difficult with her."

"Did Max make himself difficult with a lot of people?"

"Not really. You have to understand, if Max liked you, he was a big sweet pussycat. If he took a dislike to you, he would not try to hide it."

"Let's explore that for a moment, Doc."

"Mark is fine. You don't need to call me Doc or Doctor."

Frank raised an eyebrow. Would wonders never cease. "Okay, Mark, what I want to know is, were there many people recently that he might have chosen to be *difficult* with, as you put it?"

Wootten chewed that over for a while before replying.

"No, not really. Max was somewhat quieter than usual of late. I think perhaps he had things on his mind. He was subdued. I know he had some falling out with his wife Margo, I think it weighed upon him. But my point is, he didn't have his usual verve for confrontation any more in recent months. I doubt he locked horns with anybody. He seemed happiest to have a brandy with his friends, go for a long walk or work on his current article. Escapism, no doubt."

"Did he ever say much about what was going on with Margo when you would get together?"

"Something about her harassing him and accusing him of things of which he said he would be proven innocent."

"Are you aware that Margo is also dead?"

"The devil you say! No!" Wootten looked genuinely shocked. "What happened?"

It surprised Frank that news of the crime hadn't spread through the campus community yet.

"She was also murdered. I believe there's a connection."

"Murdered you say! In the same manner as Max? By the same person?"

"I don't know yet. I'm hoping you can help me. I want to come back to things he might have talked about recently, but tell me a little bit about Max and Margo, their history together."

Frank swore that Wootten's eyes misted as he began to reminisce.

"Those were the days. We were both in the Department here. In many ways it was like Never Never Land and we were the Lost Boys.

We felt like we were being paid to not grow up. We both absolutely loved literature and could indulge in it around the clock, debating it, discussing it, and of course teaching it to wide-eyed receptive students. Oh, give me some of those today. Now they can't put a decent sentence together, they have no attention spans, no interest, and they expect to get A's just for showing up."

"Um, Doc—I mean, Mark? Max and Margo?"

"Ah, I digress, forgive me. Max and I loved our work. We loved it so much that we would take it to the bar and continue to talk about it into the late hours over good whiskey. We wanted to remain eternally youthful and run with the kids.

"Max was a particularly dashing figure," he added, "— the hair style, the facial hair—even then the faculty gave him grief over that. Trendy clothes designed for people a decade younger. He tried to listen to contemporary music, read contemporary literature as well as his beloved Germans. He was worldly but youthful, brilliant but hip. He liked to hang out with students, often drank with them. I wouldn't be surprised if he smoked pot with them on occasion, but I don't know about that." He shrugged. "His students loved him. Particularly the girls."

"Margo was his student, as I understand."

"Oh yes. My, you should have seen her in those days. Full of life. Huge dreamy eyes. She was so taken by Max. He became her faculty advisor for her Master's thesis. They started to spend a good deal of time together. Shortly it was a badly kept secret on campus that they were an item."

"I can't imagine the faculty was pleased about that."

"Well, no. You have to realize, things were a bit different around here then. People could look the other way. After all, it wasn't like Margo was a child. She was a grad student, probably in her twenties. I don't think that Paula was very happy about it though."

Frank, who had been jotting in his notebook, stopped and looked up. "Paula?"

"Oh, you don't know about Paula. Of course not. That's ancient history. The woman with whom Max was living. Paula Graham."

"You're telling me Margo was the other woman, so to speak?"

"Absolutely. Max fell head over heels for her. She was young and fresh and brilliant. And considerably younger than Paula."

"And Max himself," Frank said, figuring in his head.

"Definitely. Not quite a May-December romance, more perhaps a June-October." He smirked at his own joke.

"So Paula left and Max and Margo got married."

"In a nutshell, yes. Leaving out a fair amount of soap-opera grade *sturm und drang*." More smiles at his own little humor. "Those were intense years for my friend Max."

"Very often those kinds of romances don't work out all that well," Frank said. "I mean, where the husband throws over the wife for a younger woman."

"Yes, we men are great fools in that regard, aren't we? By the way, Max and Paula weren't married. But they had been together for a number of years. During Max's earlier time here they were insepa-rable, for example at social functions and when he wasn't teaching."

"Then they grew apart," Frank suggested.

Wootten nodded.

"That had begun to happen before he met Margo. Max and Paula were very different types. Perhaps that was why Max was drawn to Margo."

"You don't think he just got dazzled by a younger woman making dreamy eyes at him?"

"Oh, she dazzled him, no question. Just as much as he dazzled *her*, when all was said and done. But what I'm saying is that Max was not a philanderer at heart. He might have found his soul mate. What he experienced with Margo was what the French would call the *coup de foudre*, the thunderbolt. He remained faithful to her for the rest of his days."

"And what about Margo, was she as steadfast?"

"I would think so. I have to admit, I didn't know her that well. We were all quite cordial with one another, just not close. After they got married, Max would spend a lot more time with her than with his colleagues, and he seldom mixed the two worlds. But I always got the impression she loved Max deeply and highly valued their rela-tionship. I don't think there was any tiptoeing through the proverbial tulips on the part of either."

Frank switched gears to see what might happen.

"What I'm interested in is if there might be anyone else who had it in for them both. Anyone come to mind for you, through the years?"

Wootten ruminated, frowned, and shook his head solemnly.

"Max had numerous run-ins on campus, but as I said, his University life never included Margo. And, well, those little donnybrooks are part of academe, and they don't as a rule lead to murders. Not that all of us might not consider it in a moment of frustration."

He smiled at Frank, noted the smile was not returned, so he continued more soberly.

"Plenty of politics and infighting, don't get me wrong. But it's not like life and death. One thing about academic types, they tend to pride themselves on being highly civilized. I would hope people keep a certain perspective."

"Returning to Paula, that was her name? Seems like she could have borne a grudge toward them both. What happened to her?"

"A sad story. She passed away, not all that long after she and Max parted company in fact, maybe a year or so."

"How did she die?"

"I'm not sure. I just remember when the word reached us of her death. She wasn't all that old. Max felt terrible. So did many of us who had known her. We were shocked."

"Did she leave any family, any relatives?"

Wootten shrugged. "Not that I know of. I think she was an only child, no siblings. She and Max didn't have any kids, of course. Max used to work for her father."

"He worked for her father?"

"Yes, when I first met him and he was working towards his doctorate, he would put in a lot of hours with her father. He was—was it a plumber? No, an electrician, that's right. Max used to love to tell me stories of crawling around under buildings and falling out of windows. That was how he met Paula."

"You don't mean by falling out a window, I assume."

"No, of course not. He and the employer got along splendidly. I remember he said the old man was a widower, loved having him around to work and talk with, said he had always wanted a son. Max liked him, said he was a great guy. Then he got some security as a teacher, working towards professorial tenure, and was able to give that up. But in the meantime he met Paula."

"And you don't know anything more about the father?"

"I heard he passed away as well, nothing more."

Frank had thought he saw a glimmer of a trail there, but it was elusive at best. Too long ago, everybody dead. Why couldn't it ever be simple? This problem was still going to have to be worried like a very tight knot.

"Okay," sighed Frank, flipping a page on his notebook. "Let's talk about the tavern companions."

The conversation with Wootten went on for nearly forty minutes.

Max was clearly a happy subject for him. He described how Max progressively gave up his flamboyant pursuit of eternal youth and embraced a more appropriate guise as a wise mentor. Max had actually chaired the Department for a couple of years before tiring of the politics and deciding to return to teaching and publishing. Immediately thereafter he had produced two amazing pieces of scholarship that were applauded in the journals.

Wootten himself had become Department Chairman and had held the position ever since. He had encouraged his old friend to continue full time, but Max had decided he wanted to dial it back of late. That finally brought them back around to the original topic.

"So it was only in recent years that Max decided to reduce his hours and started getting moody over something," Frank prompted.

"Yes. He started telling me that Margo had become strange, was growing distant to him and increasingly sarcastic. She made cryptic references. He said he had no idea what she was getting at, but she would act as if she expected he understood it. He said he was concerned she was having a nervous breakdown or early onset dementia or something along those lines."

"Just curious here: did Margo work after they got married? What did she do?"

"To my knowledge, no, she stayed at home. Max made a decent living as a tenured professor with the prestige of several highly-regarded published papers. I can't imagine Max would have minded if she had wanted to go to work, say, to teach. He always had said she was brilliant. So I have to believe that Margo didn't want to do that."

"No kids, right?"

"No children. They had a pet now and then. Max liked dogs. I suppose those were their surrogate children."

He noticed Frank's odd stare and continued, "I had two children myself. They've grown and moved away."

Frank couldn't resist asking. "Just wondering. How did your wife feel about your hanging out with Max and your other colleagues back in those days?"

"My wife *is* a colleague," he grinned. "Teaches in the Department. She even hung out with us when she could."

Frank nodded. "Anyway. All of a sudden Margo began to descend into some kind of abyss, according to Max."

"Apparently." Wootten shrugged. "All I knew were the progress reports he would bring us. He started showing up more regularly at the tavern."

"What's the name of the tavern, by the way?"

Wootten winced. "The Boar's Head. They purposely did that to attract the literary crowd. A little obvious for my taste."

Frank nodded. "Like in Shakespeare."

Wootten smiled broadly.

"You're a reader then," he commented with a nod.

"Some policemen do that," Frank admitted. "But now I'm digressing. Max. He was showing up more often at the tavern, things at home were going downhill?"

"Yes. Finally he said she had moved out. He seemed a curious mix of heartbroken and relieved. It was like that other shoe had finally fallen."

"Did he mention anything about her threatening or harassing him?"

"Oh yes, that's right. Thomas Mann was poisoned. He came home one night to find the poor thing. He loved that dog. I think it had been some solace for him after losing Margo."

"Did he mention anything else?"

"He said Margo had taken to calling him regularly, making bizarre accusations. He called her increasingly irrational."

"When I spoke with him he mentioned something about her trying to break into his condo."

"Yes, he mentioned that as well. Said someone might have jimmied his door lock or something like that, or they had come by a key illicitly. I don't think he had much of a grasp of how a lock works or what could be done to open it. We all felt he was being overly dramatic."

"But yet someone *did* poison his dog."

"Yes. I suppose that could have been Margo. If she really was losing it."

"Was Max seeing a doctor? Could he have had, say, a heart condition?"

Wootten thought this over.

"Come to think of it, he was taking some kind of pills, or at least he took some once or twice while we were together. But I have no idea what they were."

They talked for a few more minutes but it seemed to Frank he was starting to come around full circle now, and at least for the moment he was finished here.

He took the names of the two other academics who made up the "tavern companions" and bid Wootten farewell with a thanks and a handshake.

"I hope you find whoever did this horrible thing," Wootten said gravely.

"I will," replied Frank.

He wouldn't bother Monica again today. He had more questions now about Margo's married life, but they could wait.

He decided to drive back to the squad room and take stock. His mind raced as he drove. He liked to make lists in his head, and by now it was second nature for his brain to construct the lists almost subconsciously as he navigated his vehicle through traffic.

Margo could have killed Max but Max could not have killed Margo.

More likely they were both killed by the same person.

Somebody would have needed sufficient reason to kill them both.

"It's her fault." "It's his fault." What was that supposed to mean?

Both were harassing each other? Or…somebody else was harassing them both and making them think it was each other?

Why? In his mind's eye, he circled that last question over and over and over.

Something's wrong about this whole thing. You couldn't make it look as if they killed each other, that was impossible, but that's what it seemed like someone was trying to do.

Why?

Something's missing.

In frustration, Frank hit the steering wheel with the palm of his hand.

FIVE

Another of the things that amused Frank about television police shows was that police personnel never seemed to be shown actually filling out paperwork. It seemed like the major part of every real-life cop's job was doing just that. There were reasons for that, and Frank understood them well.

At some point, there needed to be a legitimate chain of evidence that could be taken to trial and not shredded by skillful defense attorneys or rejected by exasperated judges. Every officer and every detective was constantly reminded that the care they exercised in establishing that chain of evidence, documenting every interview and every action, however minor, could ultimately make the difference between conviction and acquittal.

It all made sense. He just hated it. It seemed to take up more time than everything else he did in a day.

It also meant that he could expect at least some kind of preliminary reports from the techs and the coroners, and if he was lucky he'd get something before the weekend. Otherwise he'd be out of luck until at least Monday and likely beyond.

Waiting on his desk was a large manila envelope which included summaries of the on-scene reports from Max Hesterberg's condo. He was still waiting on the autopsy and lab results, but at least this would give him something.

He dumped the pages on his desk and pored through them. Death seemed pretty clearly to be from cardiac failure as the result of being electroshocked by a Taser. No indications of forced entry, theft or vandalism. The evidence suggested that Hesterberg had opened the door to someone, who had then shot him with the Taser, watched him die, removed the darts and departed, leaving the body blocking the door.

And, Frank remembered, the attacker also left the note. IT'S HER FAULT.

He considered something, went to his computer and did a quick search. He thought he understood electroshock weapons but wanted to check to be sure. With time he was learning how useful the internet could be.

As he thought, Tasers were seldom fatal, but there still were cases of deaths from them. One study specified that a shock from a Taser "can cause cardiac electric capture and provoke cardiac arrest" and went on to describe exactly how. Wrongful-death lawsuits, he was aware, had been brought over Taser deaths. His own department was dealing with one at present.

Still, how could you be sure you'd kill somebody if you used one? Suppose you knew the intended victim had a heart condition? Would that make it a sure kill? He needed to know more about this, and made a note to consult someone.

Another thought occurred to him: what if the assailant's aim was *not* to kill Max? What if the intent was to disable him, put him out of commission for a length of time?

But if so, why?

So he would be alive when Margo was killed, perhaps somehow implicated in her death?

That seemed pretty far-fetched. Frank could find several problems with that scenario, not the least of which was those nasty burn marks on Hesterberg's chest from the darts that would provide a convincing alibi if he had survived. Things might not have gone as planned.

He shook his head. Going down this path was not productive. He needed better direction, something from the evidence. But the evidence was always slow in coming. Labs and medical examiners were always backlogged.

Sometimes it was good to be a dinosaur. He hadn't forgotten the value of the old methods. It was just that they were so tedious...

Now his desk phone was ringing, a call being put through from reception. He picked up the receiver and identified himself.

"You're the detective in charge of the Hesterberg murder?" It was a raspy woman's voice with a definite Eastern Seaboard accent.

"Excuse me, which Hesterberg murder?"

"What are you, a wise guy? What do you mean which one?"

Frank rubbed his temple with his free hand. "I'm sorry, and no, I am not being sarcastic. There are two and I'm working on both."

A short silence. "Max Hesterberg. The professor." It sounded like the husky voice of an inveterate smoker.

"Yes, how can I help you?"

"I'm his sister, Angela. I've come to town to plan his memorial service. And hopefully to get some answers from you about what the hell happened."

"I wish I could be of more help to you on that score, Miss Hesterberg..."

"Actually it's Mrs. Colletta."

"Mrs. Colletta, as a matter of fact, I'd like to see if you might be able to give *me* some information. I've only just begun the investigation and there are a lot of questions..."

"And what's this about *two* Hesterberg murders? You're not talking about..."

"His wife, Margo Hesterberg. Unfortunately, yes. She was also murdered, just yesterday."

"What the fuck!" came the exclamation over the phone. After a brief pause she said more softly, "Sorry, but just what is going on in this town?"

"I wish I could tell you. So you're in town now? Can we possibly talk today?"

"I'm here. Flew in from Pennsylvania. I'm being told Max's body can't be released so I can't plan a service yet. Is there anything you can do to help me there?"

"I doubt it, I'm sorry. They can't release him until there's been an autopsy. I'm hoping that will be done in the next few days."

"Shit, I wish that didn't have to be done." Clearly Max's sister was very different from Max himself. "Hell of a violation to Max's remains, you know?"

"I understand, Mrs. Colletta, but you can understand it's necessary in this case."

"Yeah, yeah. So I gotta play the waiting game here."

"In the meantime, it really would be a big help if you could come talk with me."

"Why not?" Angela muttered. "Tell me where I'm going."

Frank established her location and gave her directions and they agreed on an interview in an hour.

That gave him an hour to catch up on his own paper work, he decided.

Angela Colletta was a short woman with frosted hair and an expressive face. In person, her voice seemed even huskier. They were sitting in a drab interview room, drinking coffee from Styrofoam cups. Frank had apologized for the lack of amenities but she had waved it all aside.

Old school to the hilt, he was a bit taken aback by the colorfully outspoken Angela, but he was warming to her. She was clearly a no-nonsense, down to earth type, which gave him some hope of helpful insights into Max and maybe even into Margo. He had spent the first few minutes answering her numerous questions and informing her about the murder as much as he felt he could. She expressed almost equal concern as to the fate of Margo. It all seemed truly incomprehensible to her.

Frank finally decided it was time to turn the questioning around to her. "Anything you might tell me about Max and Margo's relationship?"

"Well, it's not like Max and I have been in close communication over these years. We weren't on the outs or anything, we just, well, you know. You get busy with life and don't stay in touch. Can I smoke in here?"

"I'm sorry, no."

"What the hell is wrong with the world these days, can't smoke anywhere! But anyway...I knew Margo better in the early days, when I lived out here too. She and Max seemed so much in love. She seemed to be so good for him."

"When they got married, you mean."

"And afterward. When Max met her, he was in the middle of some kind of life crisis, you know? He was approaching forty, and how he dreaded that big birthday. It, like, symbolized the end of the world for him. He was doing a lot of that shit that guys of a certain age sometimes do, you know? The clothes, the slang, everything but the red sports car! And we sometimes kidded him that that was next. I was worried when he met Margo and left his old girlfriend for her."

"That would be Paula?"

"Right, Paula Graham. I figured this was just a phase, trading her in for a younger model, a trophy girlfriend kind of thing. Only it didn't turn out like that at all. Instead they were really great for each other. For a short time they ran around doing twenty-something stuff, going to concerts, poetry readings at coffee houses, that type of thing. Then they just kind of started settling in. Max started acting more his age. She was a very settling influence, that's a good word for her."

"I'm told she was a brilliant student of literature."

"I can't speak to that, but she was smart. Quick on the uptake. Kind of innocent in the ways of the world, but articulate. Very sweet, very charming. I sorta didn't want to like her when I first met her but I couldn't help it."

"It sounds like she gave up her studies and any thought of a career to be with your brother."

"You know, it was weird. Not only did Max seem to find everything he needed in her, she seemed to find everything she needed in him. Yeah. They became like a closed circuit. They both loved books, movies, poetry—they just fit together. There was their world alone and then there was their contact with the rest of the world. Over time the two overlapped less and less."

Frank thought about what Mark Wootten had told him only a few hours earlier. The two seemed to have an idyllic marriage, at least for many years at the beginning.

"So you and Max both lived here at the time, that was about twenty-five years ago?"

"Longer. We both moved here from Pennsylvania to go to school. We established residency and went to State. Max got his degree in English and then his Masters and his doctorate. I got a degree in sociology. I decided I didn't like it out here, and it got hard to find a job. I wound up moving back near home and becoming a social worker in Philadelphia, but that was some years later."

"Max didn't go into teaching immediately after graduation?"

"Max wanted to be a perpetual student. He loved school. He went right into a grad program. He wasn't sure he wanted to teach. He wanted to write."

"So he ended up working to put himself through school, is that right?"

She laughed and made a face. "Yeah, he went to work for an electrician, Roger Graham. I swear he was going to kill himself on that job. He fell out of a couple of buildings, got a few nasty shocks, once he got stuck *under* a building and had to be pulled out by firemen! He was a *terrible* electrician. I used to call him the Electrician's Apprentice, like the Sorcerer's Apprentice, that cartoon?" Frank nodded at her. "But he took this pride in being a working man. A lot of college boys have this thing about being a working man, you know? And Roger paid him well and tolerated his incompetence."

"Paula was his boss's daughter then. And she became his girlfriend."

"I gotta tell you, I think she was a big reason that Roger kept him on the job. That plus he liked Max. He looked at him sort of like a son. Other guys who worked for him, it wasn't the same. Max was special to Roger. If I recall, Roger's wife had died; he only had Paula. He really was looking forward to Max joining the family."

"But he and Paula didn't marry, they just lived together?"

"Right. For a few years in fact. Max was getting close to his doctorate and he was offered a position at the University so he quit being an electrician before he got electrocuted, which was a good thing. Oh, shit." Angela stopped and put a hand up to her mouth.

"Mrs. Colletta?"

A tear formed in her eye. "I just realized how Max actually died."

As luck would have it, there was a box of tissues in the interview room. Frank found it and put it on the table in front of her.

"I am so fucking stupid," she said as she wiped her eyes and then blew her nose.

"No, you're not."

"I'm just mad at myself for that dumb-ass joke. Sorry for falling apart like this."

"Perfectly understandable. Take your time."

Angela recovered rapidly. No question she was a tough one. An urban social worker, Frank figured, she would have to be.

"Anyway, Max started teaching and he just took to it. He loved being around the students. As I said, by now he was in his mid to late thirties and starting to feel like he was going over the hill. He worked at his doctoral thesis for a couple more years before it was accepted. I think Roger missed having him at work but Paula was still there and they all stayed fairly close."

"Max never married Paula. No kids."

"No."

"I wonder what kept them together?"

Angela shrugged. "Never made sense to me. I'd go over to visit them and they'd just, you know, be *there*. It wasn't like they hated each other, they were always kind of happy and nice, but it wasn't like they had a lot of visible affection for each other. Max was a restless kind of guy, he wanted to do stuff. She struck me as wanting to stay at home as much as possible."

"She wasn't a student?"

"God, no. Far from it. She did work for her dad. She'd do his bookkeeping, file stuff, that kind of thing."

"So it seemed to you that Paula was more invested in the relationship than Max? You say he was starting to have this midlife crisis or whatever?"

Angela nodded with a grim smile. "Couldn't have been easy for her. I loved my brother a lot, Detective, he was a great guy in so many ways, but to be honest, he was kind of a self-absorbed sort. He made a great academic in that way."

"So Max met Margo, had a whirlwind romance."

"That was so weird. As I said, I thought that was a doomed enterprise from the outset. I thought she was this starry-eyed young bimbo infatuated with her teacher and he was this aging fool full of self-doubt whose head had been turned by his pretty young student. That's how it must have looked to everyone."

"Sounds as if they hardly acted discreetly."

"Not exactly. They were a bit of a scandal."

"So Max and Paula didn't last much longer."

"No, she had moved out and was gone and then Max and Margo were announcing their wedding."

"And what happened to Paula?"

"I don't know for sure. Moved out of town somewhere, I think, and had no contact with any of us, which is understandable. Sometime later the word got out that she had died but there were never any details. Max tried to contact Roger but he couldn't locate him. His business had closed." Angela paused for a moment and something seemed to light in her eyes. "Do you think this is important in terms of Max's death? Is that why you're asking me about all this old history?"

Frank shrugged. "I don't know, Mrs. Colletta. I'm trying to get as much background as I can. There's not an awful lot to go on. My thought is that someone bore a grudge against both Max and Margo, or maybe I should just say someone wanted them both dead. So far there's not too much I can learn about them in more recent times. I figure everything I can find out about them might be of some help."

"Well, I left town about..." she did quick computations in her head. "I think it was nineteen years ago. As I said, I lost touch with Max and Margo. But up until then I saw them on a pretty regular basis."

"Tell me a little bit about them in those years. I understand Max was a bit combative."

"You mean at work? I heard a few stories, mostly from his point of view. He was impatient with what he called truculence. That was a real Max word. I mentioned he could be self-absorbed. There were times he couldn't understand why everyone else didn't readily fall in line with his opinions on everything."

"So he had fights with other faculty members."

"If you can call it fighting. If you ask me, professorial type guys, they're all fuss and feathers. They're hung up that they're so cerebral so they feel like they have to act macho. They drink together and argue and posture and puff up like pigeons. It doesn't mean shit. It's getting out their inner machismo. I honestly could not see any of those faculty gents committing an actual act of violence. I don't know they could have had a fistfight, much less kill one another."

"I understand Max had a few run-ins with female faculty members, or administrators."

"Could be. I'm not aware of anything specific, but Max would lock horns with anybody. I was going to make a joke and say, now, women on the faculty, you better watch out, they're secure enough, they *could* be killers, but under the circumstances that's a really bad joke and I wouldn't really mean it, so I better not."

Frank caught himself rubbing the back of his neck.

Angela said, "What's the matter with me, I'm just not myself. I wish I hadn't said that."

Frank let it go but told himself that he was rather glad she had said it. It was at least a slight confirmation of one of his own few angles.

Angela could not offer much insight on Max's life for the past fifteen to twenty years, though she said she'd had a few intermittent telephone conversations with him in recent years in which he had informed her that Margo had moved out. He had been circumspect in their conversations, not volunteering much, but she had sensed his tone growing more unhappy and agitated. There was that same word again, "agitated." It seemed the term everybody who knew Max used to characterize him in recent times.

Finally Frank felt that there was no more to be gained from extending the conversation. Angela would be in town for a few more days at least, and there would be more opportunities to pursue any newer lines of inquiry. He exchanged contact information with her and asked to be informed when the service was scheduled. She thanked him for his concern, but his true interest was to see who else might show up that he might get a chance to interview.

"And by the way," she said as they shook hands, "I think I'd like you to call me Angie, okay? I've decided you're okay. And to tell you the truth, I still never got used to being Mrs. Colletta. When people call me that I look around for Vinnie's mother, you know?"

* * * *

Across the bustling squad room, Lieutenant Castillo caught Frank's eye and beckoned him into his office.

"How would you feel about overtime this weekend?" he asked. Frank shrugged. Actually he had been hoping for it.

"Why not?" he said. "Does this have to do with the Hesterberg murders?"

Castillo nodded. "Just spoke with Captain Crowley. We're getting a little bit of heat down the channels. After all it's the State University; my guess is there might be political ramifications, but you did not hear that from me. Plus it's a high profile case now. Did you happen to see the television in the last hour or so?"

"Can't say as I have."

"They found out about Margo Hesterberg and have been splattering it all over the afternoon news. It'd be best for us if we can close these murders pretty quick."

"It'd help if we could get prints, labs, coroner reports this weekend."

Castillo nodded. "I have a feeling there will be word coming down to all of them as well. But I can't promise anything. On the other hand, I know you. I can't think of anybody I'd rather have tracking this down. You've got the old-school skills."

Frank twisted one corner of his mouth up into a wry smile and said nothing. He knew this was a reference to several remarks he had previously made about younger detectives over-depending upon the science.

"So where do we stand on those cases right now?" the Lieutenant asked.

"Not all that much to go on, Lou."

It was another running semi-joke between Castillo and his detectives that they constantly called him Lou, for Lieutenant. When he first took over the office he had been just a trifle self-important and this was the veterans' way of cluing him in. He had grown in the job and earned a bit of respect by letting the little digs from his charges go by, as long as they kept the hierarchy in the proper perspective.

Frank continued. "They both thought the other was harassing them in weird ways. I'm thinking it was a third party working on both of them who then killed them both. They led very private lives, not a lot in the way of personal histories. I've got a couple of leads but I have to admit they're slim."

"Take whatever time you'd like this weekend, Frank. I got the word from the Captain directly and I can authorize whatever you need. There will be people upstairs coming in to work on Monday who are going to want some news from me. Help me out here."

An idea occurred to Frank. "Maybe I can get you to move some of my other case load over to someone else?"

Castillo eyed him carefully. "What do you have in mind?"

"Nothing all that major. I've just got these pain in the ass dead-end things that aren't going to go anywhere, we all know it, but I have to put in the time and the *due diligence* on them."

He punctuated that phrase sardonically, and then mentioned the cases by name. Castillo nodded. He knew exactly the cases to which Frank was referring. He heaved a sigh.

"You drive a hard bargain, Detective Vandegraf. Okay. Bring me the files."

"If I might make a suggestion, Lieutenant," Frank added as he started to turn around, "I think Detective Morrison is reasonably free right now."

Castillo shot him a look. "I'll take that under counsel, Detective. Good luck. Make sure I've got those files before I change my mind. And bring me something I can use Monday. Please."

He dropped his gaze to the papers on his desk, signaling they were done.

Frank returned to his desk, navigating around hectic cops bustling to and fro with purpose. He contemplated his next move. He wasn't sure what he could do, but he knew he needed to keep in motion, to put in the time and see where he found himself.

He didn't want to return to speak with Monica Wersching until tomorrow at the earliest. Give her the night, at the very least, to deal with her grief. Anyway, he wanted to mull over what he had learned today to formulate new lines of questions for her. At this point she was the only source of information about Margo.

One matter had arisen while talking with Angie Colletta. It might be easy enough to track down. He sat down at his computer and began to search out death records for Paula Graham.

He had to admit, sometimes, it was pretty great to live in the digital age. He remembered when he was a new fresh addition to the squad room and had to conduct his searches the old fashioned way, on the telephone, or by Fax, or more likely in person at the office of records. He had logged in lots of hours tracking down stray pieces of information. This method was better, much better.

He estimated the year of Paula's death around twenty-five years earlier and navigated around online pathways, chasing down possibilities. There was only one death of a Paula Graham in the area and it had occurred in the town of Amberville, a couple hundred miles to the north. That sounded promising. A few more inquiries and he had enough information to pick up the phone and request a copy of the death certificate. The records office promised to email it to him within the hour.

While he waited, he gathered together the relevant files for the cases he hoped Castillo would take off his hands and carried them to the Lieutenant's office. He made a point to walk past Marlon Morrison's desk, humming softly to himself. Morrison looked up from a book he was reading at his desk and raised his eyebrows at him. Frank just smiled and nodded at Marlon.

The death certificate came through within a half hour, which surprised Frank. He always expected bureaucracies to work slower than promised, not faster, and was seldom disappointed in those expectations.

He opened the email attachment and enlarged it on his monitor. He found himself re-reading the particulars several times, and then he printed it out, and re-read the hard copy several more times.

Now he knew how Paula Graham had died.

He cursed under his breath, not out of irritation but out of amazement. This added a whole new twist.

It was still a long shot but it was clearly the best he had.

Now he knew what he was going to be doing tomorrow.

SIX

Saturday morning, after an early start, the drive to Amberville was reasonably pleasant. It was mostly open highway, along the coast, and with a bit of a lead foot on the accelerator, he did the 185 miles in less than three hours.

Department policy mandated checking in with the local law enforcement as a courtesy, and the first thing Frank did was to search out the Amberville police.

As luck would have it, when he arrived at the reception desk he was informed that the Chief of Police herself was in the station, and he was ushered into her office. Wilma Acosta was a heavy-set woman in perhaps her mid-forties who rose from her desk to greet Frank affably. He introduced himself and showed his badge and identification, which she inspected carefully and handed back.

"How may I help you, Detective Vandegraf?" she asked, settling back at her desk and motioning to a chair for him to sit. He explained he was involved in a murder investigation and laid out his objectives as simply as he could.

She chewed over his story and nodded. "That's a good one. You're thinking this might be an important clue leading to the murderer, then?"

"To be honest, it might be nothing at all. I may have come all the way up here on a wild goose chase, Chief, and I might just be heading back home right after. Or maybe it'll lead to something. It's all I've got at the moment."

"How would you feel about my accompanying you, Detective? Not much going on around here right now, to tell you the truth, and this might turn out to be interesting. And maybe I can be of help finding your way around town."

Not exactly what he had planned on, but when he thought it over, he could think of no objections. At the very least, Chief Acosta could facilitate his search. He didn't really know what he was doing here and maybe it wouldn't be so bad to have someone to bounce ideas off of. He agreed and she stood up, grabbing her hat.

"I'd be happy to drive if that's okay."

"Why not?" said Frank. "Just let me get some things out of my car."

In a minute or two, he was climbing into Acosta's police cruiser, which was actually a late model Chevrolet Tahoe SUV.

"So what you're looking for is Amberville General Hospital," she said, putting the vehicle into gear and pulling out of the parking lot. "Right up the road here. Changed a bit since back then—you did say twenty-five years ago?"

"Correct," replied Frank, watching the road.

"But they ought to still have the records you're looking for, and maybe even someone who was there and remembers. Lots of older folk in this town."

"You seem to know the town pretty well. How long have you been Chief of Police?"

"Going on ten years now. Succeeded my husband George."

"He died?"

"Good Lord, no. Just retired. He's still sittin' at home, probably watching TV. Me, I like this job. I'll keep it as long as the people of Amberville let me."

"So you've lived here all your life?"

"Not yet," Wilma said, gunning her engine.

Shortly thereafter she announced they had arrived and pulled into a parking lot dominated by a large sign reading AMBERVILLE GENERAL HOSPITAL.

Amberville General's Chief Administrator was a cordial but businesslike woman named Alice Martin. Her office was small, tidy and surprisingly homey, with comfortable chairs and walls covered with photos. She was tapping intently at a computer; the three were seated at a small conference table. Whatever misgivings she may have had about sharing the records in question had been swept away by Wilma's friendly assurances.

Frank privately conceded that there was something to the way small towns ran. He was also glad that Wilma had come on board with him after all.

Alice swiveled the monitor screen to face Frank. He scanned what was on the screen. It confirmed what he had already learned.

"Paula Graham died in childbirth," he said simply.

"Yes, that's what our records indicate."

Frank had already done the figures in his head. Paula left Max in March. Max and Margo were married in April. Paula Graham went into her fatal labor in early October.

"She was early. Her due date had been originally calculated for late November," Alice said, peering over the top of her glasses at him.

"The child was premature. Did he or she survive?" Frank asked, trying to peruse the information on the screen.

Alice scrolled up and down. "It would seem so, yes. At least the child survived birth." She pointed to the monitor. "Baby Boy Graham, it says here. Apparently the child hadn't yet been named."

"Would there be records of the child, what happened to him?"

Alice shot a glance to Wilma, who gave a reassuring nod. She returned the screen to face her and tapped a few more keys.

"He was sent to Nightingale County Medical Center, where they had better neonatal intensive care resources. That's where our records end."

"Any indication as to the father of the child?" Frank asked.

"The father was not named."

"Did somebody bring the mother into the hospital; is that indicated?"

Alice carefully examined the information on the screen. "It would seem it was her father. He's the only other person referenced."

Wilma broke in. "How about the physician who did the delivery?"

"Let me see...here we are. Handley Lucas."

"I know Handley," Wilma said. "He's been retired for a while now. He's still in town."

"Yes. Actually his daughter took up his practice."

Wilma looked quizzically at Frank. "Think it's worth paying a visit to Handley and seeing if he remembers anything?"

"Possibly," mused Frank. He looked back at Alice. "How far away is Nightingale County Medical Center?"

"About a half hour, out Route 25. Wilma can direct you."

"I wouldn't mind starting with Dr. Lucas. Can I get a number to call him?"

"Why don't you let me do that?" Wilma said, reaching for her own phone. "Might make the whole thing go much smoother."

It didn't take long for Wilma to locate Dr. Handley Lucas or to arrange to meet with him. He was a hearty seventy-something man, still possessed of a good head of snowy hair and a warm smile. When they arrived at his home, he looked happy to greet Wilma and to be introduced to Frank. They sat at his kitchen table with mugs of fresh coffee, Frank's notebook open in front of him.

"Sure, I remember Paula," Lucas recollected. "Roger, her father, was a friend of mine. That's why she ended up in Amberville to begin with." He shook his head. "Very sad."

"What can you tell me about her, the whole situation?" Frank asked, leaning over intently. For some reason his gut feeling was telling him he was approaching something crucial to his case.

"Well, that was a long time ago. But I recall Roger calling me, saying his daughter needed a private place to bring her baby to term and then to deliver. We didn't talk about the whys and what-fors. She was in trouble and needed help. That was all I needed to know. I said of course. I found her a house for rent, she came up here, and I was her obstetrician for the course of her pregnancy."

"Paula's father, Roger—did he come with her?"

"No, but he visited her quite often. He had his business to tend to, down your way."

"You must have gotten to know her somewhat. Did you get any kind of sense of what was going on with her?"

"To be honest, I don't remember. I always had a lot of patients. Of course I tried to give them all my personal attention, but things tend to run together after so many years. And I do recall she wasn't very talkative; we never discussed much beyond her prenatal care."

"No mention of who the father of the child was?"

"No, that was something that was avoided. She refused to name him at any point."

"She went into premature labor, didn't she?"

"Specifically what happened, she had a condition known as preeclampsia. It was necessary to induce birth to try to prevent it from progressing to full-out eclampsia, which can be extremely serious, resulting in seizures in the mother and even death. The baby was delivered very early. But, as you know, the mother still did not survive."

"Was Paula's father here for the delivery?"

"Yes. He wasn't in the delivery room. We kept him out because of the complications of the procedure and the delivery, which was standard procedure. He was in the waiting room through everything."

Lucas again shook his head, this time with an expression of deep sadness even after all this time. "I had to go and tell him what had happened. It just destroyed him."

"What about the baby?"

"The baby survived, but being almost eight weeks premature, was in danger. He was transported to Nightingale to their neonatal intensive care unit."

"Do you have any idea what happened to the baby after that?"

"Oh yes," Lucas said. "He made it. Roger planned on taking his grandson back and raising him when he was out of danger. The baby had still not been named. He was just 'Baby Boy Graham' on the isolette in the NICU. Roger was going to name him Paul."

"It sounds as if something else happened before he could do that," Frank noted.

"I'm afraid so. There was an accident."

"You mean Roger Graham had an accident?"

"Yes. He was working on the wiring for a building that was under construction. He was electrocuted. Died on the spot."

"Right when he was about to bring his grandson home? Really?"

Lucas nodded sadly, briefly closed his eyes. "He was trying to finish up the job so he could devote a few days up here to all the details when they discharged the boy. Maybe he was rushed and distracted because of everything that had happened. We'll never know. He was being a bit reckless, perhaps."

Nothing much worse than a reckless electrician, Frank thought, but wisely kept it to himself.

"And the baby?"

"Nightingale County Social Services took custody. My understanding is he was put up for adoption. I have no idea what became of him. My wife and I briefly considered trying to adopt him ourselves, but we had four kids of our own. It just wasn't a viable solution."

"Did you try to follow the boy's progression?"

"It got complicated. He was transferred to somewhere else. I had some things come up here, both personal, and with my practice, that monopolized my attentions for a long time. Apparently he was adopted in the interim, and those records, as you know, are confidential."

"So it's conceivable he's a grown man today; he'd be about twenty-five."

"Oh yes."

"Would he have known about his birth mother?"

Lucas frowned. "Maybe yes, maybe no. It's possible he wound up too many steps away in the system, too many degrees of separation, so to speak. There may have been nobody who could have told him anything whatsoever. Maybe his adoptive parents never even told him he was adopted. That happens."

"He never came around here looking for information, to your knowledge?"

"No, not that I ever knew of. Sometimes I wondered about whatever happened to him. But there was really no way I could investigate."

Frank had been busily filling pages in his notebook throughout the conversation. He struggled to organize the whirlwind of thoughts and questions in his brain. "There were no other surviving relatives of the family, no close friends?"

"Not that I knew of. Roger was a widower of some years. I don't think he even had employees anymore. It was just him running the business. His daughter was all he had. And then his grandson."

"But is it conceivable that the child could have learned the back story, who his mother was, what had happened?"

"I suppose. We're in the realm of complete speculation now, Detective. People go through their whole lives never knowing anything about their birth parents or where they really came from. A lot of people these days become intensely interested in exploring those things. Some of them find out their back stories. Just as many never do. Some of it may depend upon how strong their desire is and to what lengths they're willing to go. But I tend to think it's mostly the luck of the draw."

They talked at further length and Frank asked every question he could think of. Lucas seemed willing to help as much as he could, but ultimately there was not much more he could provide. Finally Frank thanked Lucas and, with Wilma, said their goodbyes.

Outside the house Wilma told him, "You look hungry. There's a good diner not far away, want to get a bite?"

"Read my mind, Chief. Any chance they have good pastrami?"

"Corned beef okay? Their coffee's decent too. And good pie."

Frank had to admit the corned beef was good, but then he really had been hungry. They were sitting in a booth in the diner, finishing some pretty decent cinnamon-laced apple pie.

Wilma said, "You can try looking into the adoption records over at the county seat, but I think you know that's likely a fool's errand. They are *very* vigilant about that kind of thing. You'd need to get a court order—and you can get one, I'm sure—but not today."

Frank rubbed the bridge of his nose with two fingers. "I don't even know if this is really leading anyplace to begin with. It's still the best shot I seem to have so far."

"Any other promising directions?"

"Not really. The victim crossed swords with a couple of other individuals but they're not the murderous type as far as I can tell. They don't feel all that right."

"Everybody's the murderous type, given the right circumstances. That's my experience. Not yours?"

"No, you're right about that. But you know that *feel* you develop? Some things feel right for reasons you can't explain?"

"Oh sure."

"And some things don't feel right, also for reasons you can't explain."

Wilma took a sip of coffee and nodded sagely. "I've learned to trust my hunches. You do this long enough, there's something that sinks down inside you, some process. Can't explain it, can't analyze it, but more often than not it's right on the money."

"Yeah, I guess so." Frank nodded. Leave it to another cop, however far removed from him, to get the point.

Wilma continued the thought. "And something about this does feel right for reasons you can't explain, is that right?"

"Maybe it's just that I have nothing else. I don't know. I can't put my finger on it yet."

"I'd say trust your gut. And keep moving."

"I guess that's good advice. I better get going." He nodded to the waitress for a check.

"My treat," Wilma said. "This is the most interesting day I've had on the job in a while."

He thanked her, finished his pie and coffee, and figured he'd better get on the long drive home. There wasn't much more he could do here and his time was better spent there. Wilma gave him a lift back to his car at the station.

While gassing up for the return trip, he phoned Monica and asked if she was up to having another conversation with him. She seemed amenable and they set up a tentative meeting in four hours. The entire drive back down the coast, Frank allowed his brain to spin freely, giving it rein to develop patterns.

Allow certain assumptions for the moment. First assumption: Max Hesterberg was the father of Paula Graham's child.

Second assumption: Max never found out that he was a father. She learned she was in early pregnancy and left without telling him.

Third assumption: the kid survived, grew up, and discovered the story of his original parents—the whole wretched story, rife with disappointment and abandonment and tragedy.

Large jump to the scenario for the fourth assumption: many years later the son seeks out and finds his father and the woman for whom his mother was thrown over, and seeks vengeance.

He tossed the story around in various permutations and variations. There were a lot of assumptions that couldn't be substantiated. That was always a danger, to be lured off on this kind of snipe hunt without evidence.

But it was all he had so far. And something about it felt strangely right.

The trip flew by rapidly as he became fully involved in his various hypotheses. He was ten miles away from the city when he realized he didn't even remember most of the drive. It was a bit alarming to think he had been driving on automatic pilot almost all of the way.

* * * *

"I appreciate your letting me come by to talk again," Frank was saying. They were seated in Monica's living room. "How are you doing?"

"I'm not sure it's truly sunk in," she said. She seemed extremely subdued. "They won't release Margo's body yet so I can't even plan the funeral or a memorial."

"I know, I'm sorry. I hope you understand."

"I wish they didn't have to, you know..."

"Conduct an autopsy? Yes. But they do have to in a case like this."

"If it helps you to find whoever killed her," she said, "I suppose it's all for the best. Do you know how long it's going to take?"

"Maybe just this weekend, but I really don't know. It's not in my hands."

"So ask me your questions. Maybe this will help me accept the reality of it all."

"Are there any other family or friends who might be coming in for services?"

"No other relatives. Just me. Hadn't I mentioned that before? And friends, well, I'm not sure who Margo might have known. As far as I know there's only me." She laughed mirthlessly. "And those apartment managers, for what they're worth. I don't know that she had any contact with anyone else whatsoever."

"She wasn't close with them though, the apartment managers?"

"Oh heavens, no. Why would she be? I was just making a joke."

"And Margo had no contact with anyone she might have known through Max?"

"Not in a long time. I think she was suspicious of everybody that had anything to do with Max. She avoided them, I'd say."

"You said that she commented she came to believe Max was not the man she thought, something like that?"

"Yes, she said something like that quite often."

"Any idea what that might have meant? Did she find out some specific information about him, maybe something in his past?"

"She would never go into specifics with me."

"You never asked her, never pressed her on details? You weren't curious?"

"Oh of course I was, but Margo would never talk about things like that."

"Did she suspect he was having an affair, seeing other women?"

"Again, there was never anything specific. I wondered about that myself, but their history was that they both were faithful to one another. I just don't know."

"Did she ever mention anything about anybody contacting her, telling her things about Max perhaps?"

Monica thought about that one for a moment. "No, not that I can recall."

"So these just struck you as kind of free-floating concerns on her part, nothing that she had uncovered distinct details about?"

Monica pondered some more. "I keep telling you, there was something. She wasn't crazy."

"Did she ever talk about Max's life before she met him, his former girlfriend, anything like that?"

"Years ago she told me that the old girlfriend was dead, that was about it."

"No details, like how she might have died?"

"I got the feeling they didn't know. She had just disappeared, and then one day someone said she had died."

"Margo didn't really know her, I gather."

"No, she maybe met her at some social engagement once or twice. Max went to great lengths to keep them separated, I think, and that was fine with Margo. I can't imagine the old girlfriend had any interest in meeting Margo either."

"Do you think it's possible there could have been a child in Max's past? Was there anything that Margo might have said to that effect?"

"Max fathering a child? Wow! That would have been something." The idea seemed incomprehensible to her.

"I'm just throwing out possible questions, Monica. So I guess the answer to that would also be no."

"It would have been a huge surprise to me."

"So Margo wasn't always so unhappy in her marriage, right?"

"My God no, they were the happiest people together I ever saw, downright smug in their private world."

"Can you pinpoint the time when Margo started becoming concerned about Max, when she started telling you about being upset?"

"Well, it all came to a head not quite a year ago, when she moved out, but it had been building before that."

"What I'm looking for is if there was some event that triggered all this to begin with, like one day out of the blue, Margo's troubles seemed to begin."

"I can't answer that, Detective. I can't answer any of that."

The conversation ended and he thanked her. As he walked to his car, he felt the frustration with futility rising once again. It was getting late in the day and once again his wheels were spinning uselessly.

What else could it be? It had to be the child. It had to be.

He couldn't think of much else he could that evening. He could only hope tomorrow would be better.

SEVEN

It was late Sunday morning. After a fitful night, Frank had finally managed to fall asleep and to stay that way for a few hours. He was awakened by his buzzing cell phone and reached over to sleepily answer, "Yeah."

An unfamiliar male voice asked, "Hello. Is this Detective Vandecamp?"

"Vandegraf," he corrected. "Yes, this is Frank Vandegraf."

The voice was slow and thick. "Detective, my name is Gary Rossi. Angie Colletta gave me your number. She said you might be interested in hearing what I knew about Max Hesterberg."

Frank sat up in bed, now fully awake. "You knew Doctor Hesterberg?"

"Yeah, I sure did. He and I worked together for Graham Electric back in the day. I was very saddened to hear of his death. She got in touch with me when she came into town. If I can do anything to help you find who did this, I'll be glad to help."

"You might be a big help, actually. Is there somewhere we can meet?"

"Yeah, I'm near Goff Boulevard. There's a joint near here I hang out at, you want to meet me there?"

"They have food?" asked Frank. He was hungry, and it seemed early to be visiting a bar, though that was clearly what Rossi had in mind.

"Sure. Nothing fancy. Sandwiches, chili, burgers, like that."

"Reasonably quiet?"

"Usually on Sundays, yeah."

"Tell me where it is, I'll be there."

"What time is good for you?" Rossi asked.

"How about right now?"

* * * *

Frank gauged Rossi as being a bit older than Max Hesterberg would have been, a lifetime working man, wearing a denim shirt and black jeans. They met outside the establishment, which proved, as he suspected, to be a neighborhood bar. At least it was almost empty and quiet.

Rossi looked as if he had spent a lot of hours inside of bars like this. His heavy-lidded eyes had a weary quality. They found a booth and Rossi motioned to the bartender, who clearly knew him well, asking for a couple of menus. They ordered sandwiches and Rossi ordered a beer. Frank demurred on that and asked for coffee.

"You should see this place at night," Rossi smiled, as if apologizing for it.

"So, Mr. Rossi, you wanted to talk to me about Max Hesterberg."

"Yeah, I couldn't believe it when I heard what happened to him."

"You said Angie Colletta told you about it?"

"Well, actually I first heard about him on the news, on TV. Then out of the blue I got a call from Angie, who I haven't seen or talked to in, maybe fifteen, twenty years?"

"How exactly did she find you?"

"Phone book, I guess," Rossi said. "Or however you find telephone numbers these days. I still got a phone, I mean like a land line. I'm in the book or whatever it is now."

"So she remembered you."

Rossi smiled. "She used to flirt with me back in the day, when she was a smart little college girl. Had a thing for blue-collar guys, I guess. I always liked her."

"Sounds like she knew you pretty well."

He waved a hand rapidly. "Oh no, nothing like that, she was Max's little sister, we just joked around and kidded each other a little. I was married at the time, too."

"So how long did you and Max work together?"

Rossi thought about it, looking belabored. "Let's see. Roger brought him on as a helper, kind of an apprentice, when we got a spate of work and he felt he needed another hand to help out. I'd been working there for a year or two at the time. Roger really liked Max. Well, I did too. He was a good guy, made a lot of jokes but took the work seriously. Smart guy, really smart. Liked to drink, which made him popular with us too. I must have worked with him for maybe two years before I left."

"You left before Max?"

Rossi looked down at his beer and was silent for a long moment. "I sort of had to. I got arrested."

"Arrested for what?"

"Let me back up a little here. I told you I was married? Well, we had a few arguments. A few fights. I was going out and drinking a bit too much. I got in a couple barroom fights and got hauled in. Someone swore out an assault complaint against me. Roger decided he had had enough with me and he fired me after that."

Frank just nodded.

"Uh, I'm not sure that Angie knows that part, don't tell her, okay? She just remembers me as this nice friendly guy who used to kid around with her."

"No problem."

"Anyway, after I settled all that legal stuff and went through a divorce, I found another job as an electrician and sometime later Roger and I got to be friends again. Bygones and all that. He wouldn't hire me back but we'd sometimes get together for a beer. Once, we even went to a ball game."

"You say you knew Max for a couple of years. Tell me what you remember about him."

"He would tell me how he was working on his degree, writing his thesis, he called it? He loved to read; he'd constantly tell me about some book or writer. I kinda got a kick out of it. Usually those egg-head types look down their noses at people who actually work for a living, you'd go to do a job for some *professional* and they'd talk down to you and watch you like they didn't trust you weren't gonna steal something, stuff like that? Max wasn't like that. He was real people. I could see he was gonna go someplace, as they say."

"Did you know much about his personal life?"

"I knew he and Roger's daughter had hit it off and they were going out. She was kind of a strange bird."

"How do you mean?"

"Well, she was pretty cute, certainly nothing wrong with her on that score, but I don't think a lot of guys showed much interest in her, at least not past maybe a date or two. She was real shy. She finished high school and took a year at community college, but she wasn't much of a student, I guess. Roger had her working for him, keeping the books and taking phone calls and like that, so she was in the office a lot.

"That's how she and Max got to know each other," he added. "I think Roger was tickled to death that she liked Max and he liked her. He might have been worried that she was some kind of wallflower who would have ended up alone. Roger really liked Max. I think he was looking forward to having him as a son-in-law."

"Was it while you were there that Max and Paula moved in together?"

"Oh yeah. I kidded him about that. At first Roger wasn't real happy with that arrangement but he saw that Paula seemed happy with Max, so I guess he decided it would be okay."

"I hear Max wasn't much of an electrician."

Rossi laughed loudly, the most energy he had so far displayed. He shook his head as if recalling a favorite joke.

"At heart he was a college boy," he said, clearly with affection. "Roger sure didn't keep him on for his skills. He was never going to be a certified electrician. There were only certain things he was allowed do as an uncertified assistant, and he still managed to almost kill or seriously injure himself a few times."

"Roger knew Max was going to leave one day. He was working on his doctorate."

"Yeah, of course. Max never misled him on that score. They were honest with each other."

"Until they weren't." Frank watched Rossi carefully.

Rossi just shrugged. "I was long gone by the time all that happened. I later heard the story from Roger when we reconciled."

"What was Roger's take on everything?"

"Max got offered a job as a teacher of some kind and quit. Roger was okay with that because Max would still be like in the family. Roger was very proud of Max and would brag about him to everyone he knew. He was still figuring they'd get married, have kids. Then Paula told him that she thought Max was seeing another girl. Stuff started happening real fast, they had some blow-up fights and Paula left. That was the story." Rossi spread his hands.

"Did Roger ever tell you what happened after that?"

"Yeah. She was pregnant."

Frank was dumbfounded for a long few moments.

"You knew about that?"

"Sure. One night Roger and I got fairly drunk and he told me."

"I didn't know that anybody actually knew about that."

"I don't think he ever told anybody else. Like I said, he was pretty wasted. I don't know if he even remembered ever telling me."

"What else did he tell you?"

"Just that she didn't want to tell Max so he sent her off somewhere to have the baby. That's all I know. I made a point of never bringing up the subject again with Roger. We only saw each other a few more times before he died. You know about that, right?"

"I heard it was an accident."

"Yeah, story I got was he was up in this new construction and got killed. I hadn't seen him in a while, heard the word one night. Too bad. I later heard that his daughter had died too, but that was a vague kind of a rumor, I never learned if it was true."

"And you never looked into it?"

"Well," Rossi spread his hands, "to tell you the truth, I got myself in some more trouble right about then. I had kind of a full plate, if you know what I mean."

"Back to jail?"

"Coupla fights, drunk and disorderly, I spent a little time in jail. Not prison, not the penitentiary, nothing like that. Just piddly-shit stuff. After that, I just got out, moved on. Decided to keep my nose clean and work. Got married again."

"How'd that work out?"

"And divorced again."

"Sorry."

"And married again and divorced again. It's like lather, rinse, repeat." He looked sad and weary, like an aging basset hound.

"Mr. Rossi, did you ever tell anyone else about Paula, about her pregnancy, any of that?"

"No, I thought it needed to be kept private out of respect for the dead. In fact I kinda forgot about it. Oh. There was just that one guy."

Frank almost dropped his pencil. "What one guy?"

"About maybe two years ago? Guy calls me out of the blue and asks if I used to work for Roger Graham. Says his father was an old friend and he just wanted to find out what had happened to him."

"How did he find you?"

"Search me. I figured Roger had mentioned me to the guy's father way back when. It was all kinda vague."

"You didn't ask who he was or anything?"

Sheepish grin. "Well, I guess I had been drinking a little bit."

Frank resisted the urge to bury his face in his hands. "And what exactly did you tell him?"

"I got caught up in talking about old times. I guess I told him the whole story, what I knew of it. He seemed really interested, said his father would have been very upset to learn his friend was dead. He asked me about working with Roger."

Frank took a deep breath. "You told him about Paula being pregnant?"

"I might have. Don't really remember."

"You told him about Max."

"Yeah, probably."

"You told him about Max leaving Paula for a new girlfriend?"

"I might have, I don't remember. We were just talking, you know? Maybe gossiping a little."

Frank could see that even after one beer Rossi was quickly getting a little sloppy. He could imagine him after "drinking a little bit."

"And you have no idea who this guy was? Who this father he was talking about might have been?"

"Like I said, I had been drinking. It was a real friendly conversation, the guy was very, whattaya call it, engaging? It was like we had met up in a bar, even like this one." He waved around the room grandly.

Then he looked morose again. The slouchy hangdog look returned. "That's maybe why I remember anything about it. I miss stuff like that. Not a lot to laugh about these days. Not a lot of good memories to share about old friends. That was a fun conversation. I invited the guy to come join me for a drink but he said he had to get going, maybe some other time."

"Good memories," muttered Frank.

"Sorry, missed that, what'd you say?" Rossi said.

"Nothing," replied Frank. "Did this guy happen to give his name?"

"Don't remember," Rossi said with a weak smile. "I had been..."

"I know," said Frank, shutting his notebook. "Drinking." He started to get up. "Thank you for your help, Mr. Rossi."

"You know, I'm thinking I know why Angie got in touch with me," Rossi said. "I think she wanted to get together, you know what I mean? She said something about a husband back in Jersey or Pennsylvania or someplace. I think she wasn't in a hurry to get back to him, get my meaning?" He tried to wink but was even having trouble with that.

As Frank departed the dingy neighborhood saloon, he thought: there are smart people. There are stupid people. And then there's Gary Rossi.

* * * *

He sat in his car mulling it over. It was becoming increasingly clear. He had to get those adoption records and there was no way to get them on a Sunday.

In this state, law enforcement agencies generally were able to obtain copies of most public records, but adoption records were different. They were sealed after an adoption was finalized and usually could only be accessed by a court order. He could get one, but the process would take a couple of days.

He had a feeling he didn't have much time. The murderer would likely not hang around for very long, if indeed the murderer was even still here. For all he knew, the window of opportunity had already closed.

Once again his phone buzzed and he dug it out to answer.

"You know, your voice is deeper on the phone than in person, Detective."

"Chief Acosta, what a surprise."

"You can call me Wilma. Can I call you Frank?"

"Wilma, if you're calling with some kind of news, you can call me anything you want."

"So I didn't get you at a bad time. Glad to hear it. I took a little trip over to the city of Nightingale last night and asked around a bit. Figured you wouldn't mind, and things are pretty quiet here."

"I only wish things ever got that quiet here."

"City mouse, country mouse, you know that story?"

"Sure."

"Anyway. I've got friends who work in the hospital and at the courthouse. Hunted down a pretty remarkable lady, she must be ninety. Her name's Helen Troy."

"Helen of Troy? That would make her old indeed."

"No 'of,' wise guy. Just Helen, space, Troy. She worked in Social Services for most of her life. She actually remembered Baby Boy Graham."

"You gotta be kidding me."

"Well, here's the thing. She arranged the adoption. For her in-laws."

"Tell me you're making this up!"

"Small towns, Frank. Everybody knows everybody. Everybody winds up related to everybody. You come up to a place like this to get lost, but what you do is get known."

"Do I need to come back up there?"

"Naw, not worth it. I can tell you the sum total of what I was able to learn. It's not like she could tell me a whole lot. Just enough, I hope."

Frank had his notebook out at the ready. He was almost trembling with excitement and had to catch himself.

"Baby Boy Graham was adopted by Joseph and Anna Benecke. They lived in the city of Nightingale." She spelled it for him.

"You say they're this lady Helen's in-laws?"

"Were. Past tense, they are gone, may they rest in perpetual light. Not close relatives. Her husband didn't get along with his sister—that was Anna. It would seem that Joe and Anna were decent enough but a little eccentric and kind of a pain to get along with."

"And they adopted the boy?"

"Yep. Helen said the kid's name was something like Arnold or Ernie or Emile or something like that. That's really all she had. Helen's reasonably sharp for a nonagenarian, but she tends to ramble. I had to sit through a lengthy recitation of her family tree and friends and their friends, all sorts of side trips to get that much."

"What happened to them? Any idea?"

"She's positive, they're dead. She has no idea what became of the kid. He'd be about twenty-five now."

He scribbled furiously on the notebook in his lap. "I'd guess anything else I need to search for, I can do from here."

"That's kinda what I figured. So calling you Frank is OK then?"

"Wilma, I owe you big. I'll come up and buy you dinner some night."

"Just don't tell George, my husband. Talk to you later."

Frank started his car. His next destination was the squad room, his computer, and maybe even old-fashioned telephone books, anything at his disposal. With luck he just might be able to access information, even on a Sunday, for people named Benecke in that area.

It could drive him nuts but this digital age wasn't such a bad thing after all, he considered. He sat at his desk staring at his computer screen. The squad room was fairly quiet at the moment, only a few detectives on duty around the station.

It took some time navigating around and following one lead to the next—he was still not totally adept at this—but he lucked out. The name in front of him, and the recently added post office address, could have had a flashing neon marquee around it and would not have stood out any more to him. Things clicked into place in his mind.

He grabbed his car keys and got to his feet.

* * * *

"Detective, don't you ever take a day off over there at the police department?" Super Judy stood in her doorway and stared with some vexation at Frank.

Inside the apartment, over her shoulder, he could see her husband Steve sitting on the sofa with a beer, watching the television and casting annoyed glances over to the doorway.

"Sorry to disturb you, but I just have a couple quick questions for you."

"Well, let's get it over with, then."

"The other day when I was here you had a guy helping you out. I think he was moving the trash bins out to the street."

"Yeah, Emil. What about him?"

"Do you happen to know his last name?"

Judy shook her head. "Yeah, it's, uh...hey Steve!" she called out. "Emil's last name, it's like Becker or...?"

"Benecke, maybe?" Frank interrupted.

"Yeah. That's it. Why?"

"How do you know him?"

"He came around looking for work one day, just rang our bell, said he was going all over the neighborhood since he'd just moved in close by. He's real handy. Good worker. Steve said he'd hire him on a job by job basis."

"How long has he been working for you?"

"Oh, let me think. Less than a year, I'd say."

"Could you connect it to something else to pin it down? Say, maybe, was it after Margo Hesterberg moved in here?"

"Definitely after that. One of his first jobs was to help us dispose of the stuff we took out and stored when we cleaned out the garden apartment to rent it."

Steve had gotten up from the couch and joined Judy at the door. He hadn't let go of his beer. "You're asking about Emil? Is he in trouble or something?"

"I just need to find him to talk to him. What do you know about him?"

Steve shrugged. "Quiet guy, doesn't talk much. Pretty smart. Knows how to do all sorts of things. He didn't have a résumé or anything like that, but he told me he worked in a hardware store, as a locksmith, as a watch repairman, as a general handyman. He was even a building manager once."

"Ever talk about his personal background? Where he's from, anything like that?"

"He doesn't talk about himself much, but he did say he was from somewhere up north. He remarked he wasn't used to a big city like this one."

"Do you have an address for Emil?"

"I'm not sure," Steve said, looking dubious.

"He works for you, you have to pay him, you have to have information for him. You have to be able to get in touch with him to come over when you need him."

"Well, we usually pay him in cash. But yeah, let me look." Steve walked into the kitchen and returned with a card that might have been tacked on a bulletin board or stuck to the refrigerator with a magnet. It was covered with scrawls in pen. "Yeah, got his number and an address."

"I'm going to need this," Frank said, taking the card. It bore a cell phone number with an out-of-town area code: the same code, he recalled, as Nightingale County. There was also an address, only a few blocks away.

"I'll need that back," Steve said.

Frank just nodded. If he was right, Steve and Judy wouldn't be using the card anymore, but he saw no need to mention that. "Emil hasn't said anything about leaving town or anything like that, has he?"

Judy, who had been taking all this in with her eyes and mouth agape, shook her head. "He's supposed to help us do some painting starting tomorrow. And as soon as we get the okay from you guys, we're going to start clearing out the garden apartment to re-rent it."

Frank gave the address another look and pocketed the card. He looked at them both, trying not to show his excitement. "Thanks for your help. No big deal going on, I just need to ask Emil a few questions. Enjoy the rest of your Sunday."

He hustled back to the elevator and out to his car.

It made too much sense. It had to be the guy. Frank had noted that Emil had even worked as a locksmith.

The only thing he couldn't figure out was why Emil was still hanging around. If he had committed the murders, why wasn't he in the wind?

Did he need to get back into the apartments? They were both sealed crime scenes at the moment. He must also be confident that nobody knew who he was, so he felt that he had time. Maybe that was it. He had to feel his work was done, didn't he? He had agreed to come back to work tomorrow. Why hadn't he run yet?

"Pretty smart," Steve had characterized him. "The guy knows a lot."

Frank was familiar with a particular type of killer along this line. He prides himself on his intellect. He figures he's several steps ahead of all of us and doesn't have anything to worry about, no need to hurry. He can safely lag back and savor watching us spin our wheels.

The kind of guy with the audacity to leave a calling card at each of his murders, IT'S HER FAULT and IT'S HIS FAULT.

A man capable of two cold-blooded killings.

Frank picked up his phone and called for backup at the address.

EIGHT

In a cramped apartment, a lone man sat pensively in a darkened room, the only source of light coming from a television screen. The shades were drawn tightly against the outside world though he assured himself he felt no fear whatsoever. Nobody out there could hurt him. They didn't even know who he was. But despite his self-assurances, he was nervously trembling.

The television news (which seemed to always be on *some* channel or other, no matter what time of day or night) was still featuring breathless reports on the two shocking murders of the previous week. A series of big-haired, bubble-headed personalities stressed that the police seemed to have no clues or information on the identity of the murderers, though there was speculation they were connected.

He found it interesting that there was no mention of the notes that had been left. Certainly they had found them. He had read that they—the police—liked to withhold certain evidence from the public, as a way of counter-checking the veracity of wannabe witnesses or those crazy people who just wanted to confess to crimes they had nothing to do with. That must be what was happening now, he figured. People, he reflected, could certainly be deranged.

He had been monitoring the news regularly to see if anyone was on to him. Not that he thought they ever would be. He had been clever. His plan had been perfect, if he did say so himself. They'd never figure it out.

Tomorrow, he'd check his post office box. His regular check ought to be there as it always was on Mondays, and he could leave. He was still considering where he would go next. Not back home. There was nothing there for him anymore; it was no longer *home*. He'd go somewhere far away.

His current thought was Florida. He liked the pictures he had seen—all those palm trees and beaches. With all of his skills, he could get a job there and between that and his regular checks, maybe save up enough to go to Europe. He'd always wanted to see Europe.

He wondered why he didn't feel better, now that he had accomplished what he had set out to do. For so long now, it had been eating away at him as he planned it and took each step so carefully. How many times had he almost lost patience, been tempted to throw caution to the winds and act impetuously, just so that those gnawing feelings in his guts would go away? But he was too smart for that. He had forced himself to calm down and go slowly.

Why didn't he feel better now? he wondered. He felt terrible. The stomach ache was still there, the shaking apprehension all over his body.

He was right, the signs were right. It was all their fault and he had taken care of that. The fear, the aches should all have gone away as he was utterly convinced they would. Dad had always taught him to stay calm, think before he acted, think thoroughly, plan for every eventuality. Dad always promised that would always lead to success. Dad taught him to investigate, to learn precisely how things worked, to be methodical in his approach: how to navigate the intricacies of watches, of locks, of all manner of machinery.

But of course that wasn't really his Dad. Maybe, then, everything he had taught him was wrong.

He remembered finding out that they weren't his parents. They told him not long before they died. He remembered how it turned his life upside down, changed something inside of him.

It had taken a long time but he had pieced together his own story, the hidden history that he had been forbidden to know until then. It infuriated him that he had been kept in the dark all those years. No, he had been *lied* to, by people he trusted.

So of course they deserved to die. They were old, he just sort of helped them along.

He wished he had known his real mother. He had come to picture her in his mind: beautiful, wise, kind and loving. She would never have lied to him, never. She was a martyred saint. Her very love for him, her son, had killed her.

He wished he had known his grandfather. He had a mental picture of him as well: ruggedly handsome, long-suffering, and supportive. Had the two of them only lived, his only real family, what a life he could have had!

It was not their fault they had died, his mother and grandfather. He had learned that in his journey as well. The procedure worked: investigate, observe, learn how things work. Wait until you know everything. It was a slow process, small steps, discovering the names of his mother and grandfather, tracing them back to the city. He was intensely proud of himself for unearthing the information about Roger Graham's business, tracking down an old employee, playing his role perfectly, and learning the key information that had led him to his birth father.

As he learned things, he put it all together logically: his father had abandoned his mother for some younger trollop. They both still lived in the same city, the very place that the betrayal of his mother had taken place. His plan practically sprang to life fully developed. He moved there, set up a post office box so he could receive his weekly checks from the modest inheritance that had been left him.

The rest was easy: painstakingly methodical, but easy. He proudly envisioned himself as a kind of Ninja secret agent, slipping in and out of both their lives undetected. He had been right under their noses; sometimes they had actually seen him and passed by him without a clue that he was their righteous nemesis. He learned all about them.

He started with the woman, his father's silly harlot: there was something about her, some kind of vibration he could sense, that told him her innermost secrets. She was emotionally unsteady, he could feel it. Not surprising in such an evil presence, he judged. Evil was always, at heart, weak. He began to subtly work on her perceived weakness, to leave her deliberately obscure phone messages suggesting her husband was not what he seemed and so forth. Sure enough, she began to come apart.

That was his first objective, to sow torment, confusion and insecurity. When she moved out of the condo, as he knew she would, his plan kicked into the next gear. He followed her to her new apartment and set himself up close by. He approached the building managers and talked them into a job. Again he played his role to perfection. He charmed them into trusting him, making it simple to slip into their quarters and get the keys to the garden apartment.

So began his campaign to undermine her completely, slipping into her place, conspicuously breaking and moving things like some vengeful poltergeist. Finding the photographs was an extra reward for him. He had spent a dangerously long time paging through those— always wearing his latex gloves, of course, for he was always smart and careful—before he left them out as a message. Mementos from the past, from the time when she stole his father from his mother. Whether she grasped the message or not was irrelevant. Leaving them out was the whole point.

Getting into his father's place was a bit trickier, but he had been smart and careful. He learned the flow of the occupants, followed his father (a man of exacting habit, fortunately, and very predictable) until he knew his schedule down cold. He could predict when the floor was empty, the coast was clear, and began to perform subtle mischiefs, escalating as he proceeded. He especially enjoyed poisoning the dog. He had never liked dogs.

Then came the long-awaited endgame.

He stepped up his campaign against his father's silly harlot until, as he had predicted, she fled her apartment in terror. He was watching her diligently, easily followed her to the hotel and realized everything was in place. It was time to culminate his smart and careful plan.

He made a quick call to his father and said simply, "I'm your son. I'm coming over to tell you the story."

He knew the twelfth floor was deserted and would remain so for long enough. His father opened the door without hesitation. His one regret was that he had instantly died from the Taser gun: he had hoped to simply stun him, drag him inside, and finish the job with his garotte, then perhaps search for photos or memorabilia. But brilliant planners improvise, after all. He wore gloves, left no prints, left only the card he had printed out the night before on one of the computers available at an instant printer. He purposely left the door ajar and fled when he heard the elevator coming.

Someone was coming home early.

By this time he'd begun to work himself into a rage. Something about the living purity of his anger, the newness and the intensity of it finally unleashed, actually felt good to him. He savored it, letting it build and build as he drove to the hotel.

He knocked on the harlot's door, saying he was a maintenance person, and the stupid woman let him right in! His fury was so pure and fierce, it was hard to remember what followed. But he knew he had been smart and careful. He had even waited long enough to undo the cord and leave the note.

This time he had hand printed it. Different but similar. That would throw them off. And he thought it a nice touch to leave the maid sign on the door as he departed.

He had a wonderful, reassuring clarity about everything. The authorities were stupid; he was smart. By the time they figured out anything, he would be long gone. All he needed was the last check. No notice or farewells to anyone, he would just leave. He would pack his car tonight.

So why was he trembling uncontrollably?

He turned off the television and considered the terrible anxiety clawing at his insides: once he was on the road, away from this monstrous city that had destroyed his mother and his life, maybe it would all start to feel better.

Maybe his check had come yesterday and he could leave sooner, cash it somewhere on the road. He hadn't checked the mail this weekend. The area with the lock boxes was usually left open by the Post Office on the weekends. Maybe it was worth going over to check it out. Perhaps what was driving him crazy was the inaction, the waiting.

He decided to walk over right now. At the very least it was something to do, to occupy his time.

NINE

Frank had only seen him one time for just a few moments, but Emil looked as he remembered him from that brief encounter: lean but muscular, short dark hair, clean shaven, a fairly ordinary looking young man in dark shirt and jeans.

Downright nondescript. He may have deliberately avoided any physical characteristics, like a beard or mustache, that would make him noticeable.

He was leaving his apartment house, a low brick building on a narrow street in a neighborhood one would hardly describe as upscale. Frank had just parked his car across the street when he saw Emil coming out the doorway directly onto the sidewalk, turning to his right. He seemed to be preoccupied, taking long strides without paying much heed to his surroundings.

Frank looked up and down the street. No officer backup yet. He couldn't wait. He was out of the car, on his feet and calculating an angle to cross the street and intercept his quarry. He reached under his jacket to the service automatic he kept in his shoulder holster and kept his hand there as he walked.

Emil was still seemingly oblivious to his immediate environment, walking fast. Frank checked the street for traffic and began to cross, angling in on him.

Suddenly there was the sound of brakes and the blare of a car horn. Frank looked up to see a car pulling out of a parking space driven by a young woman who had been looking in her mirror, not to her front. She was just about to accelerate right into him before seeing him at the last minute, and now she was yelling something at him.

Frank cursed under his breath. He looked up to see Emil, about ten feet away, staring right at him. For a moment he froze as they looked at each other. Recognition dawned in the young man's eyes and he turned to run.

Hang the luck. He hated chases.

He yelled out, "Hey Emil! Hang on! I just want to talk to you!" even as he broke into a dash as best he could.

He wasn't kidding himself here. Emil had more than a couple of decades on him and he didn't think he had much of a chance of catching him in a chase. He was going to lose him and probably never find him again, now that he had been tipped off. The advantage would be forever lost. He could see Emil expanding the distance between them even as they raced down the block, and he thought he heard sirens not far away.

Frank considered drawing his weapon and announcing he would shoot if Emil did not stop. He knew Emil would not stop and he would have to shoot. In the split second before he made his decision, fate intervened.

The way Frank would later tell the story: "Well, not exactly fate, it was a squad car that intervened."

At the intersection, Emil shot into the street, not slowing his pace nor looking in either direction. There was a scream of brakes. Frank, bringing himself to an abrupt stop, could not help but see Emil Benecke flying up onto the blue and white hood of a police cruiser that was screeching to a halt on the pavement. Suddenly Frank was very much aware that there were indeed sirens, and they were all around him.

TEN

"Lucky perp," Lieutenant Castillo was remarking. "He could have been badly injured, even killed." His voice suggested that he wasn't exactly relieved at this turn of fate.

There were those cynics among the force that would have happily suggested that such a course would have been preferable, saving the city an expensive trial and ensuring that justice had indeed been served. Frank was not one of those.

"A few bumps and scratches, some bandages. I'd say he was lucky indeed. Me too. I was about to draw my weapon on him. I knew that if he got away from me, he'd be in the wind for good."

Castillo nodded seriously. "Always a bad thing when you have to fire your weapon, especially if it's fatal. And shooting in the back, that's worse. Inquests, all sorts of stuff, put you on leave while it's investigated, all that."

Not to mention, thought Frank, the death of another human being on my shoulders. It would not have been the first death at his hands and the odds were such that it would not be the last. Sometimes it had been utterly necessary. That unfortunately came with his job. But he didn't want another one if he could help it. Certainly not this way. It seemed to him that Castillo felt differently.

"Is he talking?" Castillo asked. Frank shrugged.

"He said he didn't want a lawyer. I guess he thinks he's smarter than any of them. My guess is he'll talk before long, and my other guess is he's going to be found mentally unsound."

Frank turned out to be correct on both counts. Emil Benecke would tell his tale and a court would find him unfit to stand trial. The entire far-fetched scenario would gradually come to light and cause more than one detective to shake their head in amazement. Emil would ultimately be remanded to an institution for the remainder of his life, with no chance of ever seeing the outside world again.

Ultimately, all those left behind would have to find some kind of closure in their own lives.

Once he did begin to talk, Emil wouldn't shut up. He insisted that the world know his story. He dictated a lengthy manifesto to his interrogators. Everything, to him, had a logic that he said was "glaringly clear." When he was asked about his choice of weapons, Emil was forthright. His grandfather had died by electrocution. Somehow he had come to believe that his mother had suffocated to death in childbirth. He also had come to see the disappointments of his own life in terms of being suffocated and then shocked. He said there was a "symmetry" that Max and Margo should die by electrocution and strangling.

A search of Emil's residence turned up the Taser, an impressive set of locksmith tools and picks, and even a set of Sharpie permanent markers, the kind that had been used to create the sign left on Margo Hesterberg's body. It would have been a slam-dunk case for any prosecutor, Frank would later consider, excepting for the fact that the defendant was totally bonkers.

Frank decided he had a few more loose ends to tie up on the cases before moving on. As he left Castillo's office, he passed Marlon Morrison, who gave him a pat on the back and said, "Great job, Frank. I knew I gave that to the right guy."

Frank couldn't help noticing that Marlon was carrying a thick and familiar file and wasn't looking very happy as he trudged to his desk.

* * * *

"The coroner will release the body tonight," Monica said. They were once again sitting in her front parlor, this time with cups of tea on the table in front of them. "Thank you for all your help, Detective. Will you be at the memorial service day after tomorrow?"

"I'm not sure, Ms. Wersching. Demands of the job and all. I'll try to be there though."

In reality he hoped to avoid either service, now that the cases had been resolved. There was something about all these people that bothered him.

Earlier that day he had talked to Angie Colletta on the phone and conveyed basically the same answer, that he would try to make the services for Max but might not be able to be present. They talked briefly about Max and his memory, and then he had asked her about Gary Rossi. Specifically he was curious: why had she neglected to mention him in their own conversation but then had referred him to Frank after the fact?

"Well, can I level with you, Detective?"

"Sure."

"I had these memories of Gary, you know? From when I was much younger and a student? And he was this kind of flirty, hunky older guy, the whole working man thing with the tool belt and all? I kind of thought, maybe I could look him up and see if he resembled my memories?"

It bugged him when somebody started turning every statement into a question by raising their voice at the end, but this wasn't his story being told.

"Uh huh," mumbled Frank, rubbing the back of his neck.

"He wasn't that hard to find. Still in the book." She paused, probably to take a puff from her cigarette, and continued in her throaty voice. "Frank—may I call you that, because I find this hard to say if I'm calling you Detective? Frank, I gotta tell you, me and my long-time hubby, we have kinda grown apart just a little? Here I was stuck here for who knows how long, I'm bored and restless, are you following me? I just thought I'd look into him, what was the harm?"

He contributed another "Uh huh," as if he were monitoring a confession in an interview room. It was feeling like that all of a sudden.

"Well, I met up with him, and, let's just say you can't go back, you know?"

"I know."

"I felt this sudden wave of shame and embarrassment that this old sad, sloppy drunk was the object of my little-girl fantasies and that I was entertaining any ideas however slight of fooling around on my Vinnie back home. My life's not perfect but it's actually not bad, you know? And I suddenly missed my job and my guy. So I told Gary he should get in touch with you and gave him your number, I figured that gave me an excuse and an out. And I got the hell out of that shithole bar."

"I bet I even know which bar."

"Sorry to inflict him on you."

"No, actually he was of value."

"We all should be, Frank," Angie coughed. "We all should be."

* * * *

He snapped back to the present and realized he had missed the beginning of what Monica was telling him.

"...so I think maybe once that's done I might move on."

"I'm sorry," Frank said a bit sheepishly. The observant, ever-vigilant detective caught daydreaming. He shook his head as if to clear the cobwebs, causing Monica to smile. "So you say you're leaving town?"

"As soon as Margo's put to rest and her things are put in order. There are too many bad memories here and no real reason for me to stay. I'll keep a few of her mementoes and, as I said, move on."

"Where will you go?"

"I'm not sure. I've got money saved. Maybe it's time for an adventure: a new town and a new beginning. I got to thinking that Margo and I tended to sit around way too much. Maybe I can travel then find a place with some part time or volunteer work with someone not afraid to take on an elderly lady like me."

"You're not that old," Frank said.

"I'm ancient," Monica laughed. "That won't stop me." Then she changed the subject.

"That demented lunatic man," she said sadly. "I feel badly for him, even after what he did. He must have been so tortured inside."

"The whole story may never come out. It seems his stepparents did the best they could but they were sort of loopy to begin with. And they never told him the truth about his real mother."

"He played upon my sister's insecurities. He drove her to a kind of insanity, as much as I didn't want to believe that, and destroyed her marriage. I ended up hating Max too. That—*monster*—destroyed us all. I should want to watch this Emil Benecke drawn and quartered."

She looked up at Frank, her chin held high in a curious pose of nobility. "But I don't. I'm angry, yes, but mostly, I just feel this horrible pity for him. Isn't that strange?"

"No, it just proves your humanity, Monica."

They chatted a bit further. Frank took a last sip of tea, thanked her for the refreshments, stood up and wished her good luck.

As he walked out the door he knew he would likely never see her, or Angela Colletta, again. That was all for the best.

By the time he was in his car he was trying his best to flush away the uncomfortable feelings he felt from the Hesterberg cases. He had dealt with much worse, and had always walked away with some vestige of sanity, if not serenity. This one would pass too.

A human being's seemingly unlimited potential for inhumanity never ceased to affect him, he reflected. Moving on and leaving the demons behind was never easy, and sometimes he didn't entirely succeed.

But, as he had just advised Monica Wersching, perhaps that just proved his humanity.

THE OTHER FRANK

ONE

"Do you mean to tell me, Frank, that you are actually taking some of your vacation time? Am I dreaming here?"

Detective Frank Vandegraf looked across the cluttered desk at his Lieutenant, Hank Castillo, and shrugged. "Technically, Lou, I'm taking personal time, not vacation time. But, yeah. Is there a problem?"

"A problem?" Castillo mused, a bit of a smile twitching the corners of his mouth. "No, of course not. I just wasn't sure I heard you right. You pretty much never take your time, Frank. It's actually become a bit of a problem with Personnel, just how much you've accrued. Are you feeling all right?"

Frank reached up to rub the back of his neck and then stopped himself. He was constantly being kidded about that involuntary gesture. "I'm fine. It's just that I need to go out of town for a few days. A funeral and all that kind of thing."

"Somebody close to you, I assume?"

"My ex-wife, Muriel."

"Oh yes." Castillo nodded. "I remember her. I'm sorry. Was it unexpected?"

"Apparently she had an accident. They called me this morning. Small town in the Midwest."

"I get the impression you hadn't stayed very close with her all these years."

"Um…no. She moved back to her hometown, met some guy there and remarried. Hadn't heard from her in years."

There was an awkward silence. Frank shrugged. "And clearly I won't after this either."

"Maybe this is a good thing to be doing, then. Sounds like you decided you need to go."

Frank nodded, lips pursed. "Yeah, well…I just figured, well, I've got the time and all."

Castillo continued to nod sagely. He was a muscular man, whose thick eyebrows, salt-and-pepper mustache, and graying temples all lent him an air of gravitas. As usual he had his suit jacket off but could still look dapper in shirt, tie, and vest.

He looked down at the forms Frank had handed him. "So you're departing tomorrow?"

"Got a flight out first thing. I'll be back next week."

"Works for me, Frank. Good luck. You have a few things open, I believe."

"Nothing really pressing anyway, just some pain in the neck re-canvasses and so forth. I'm happy to hand them off if you'd like."

"I think that's wise. Unless I'm mistaken, Morrison is up right now."

Frank suppressed a smile. Both he and Castillo understood that Detective Marlon Morrison was almost always unoccupied. He was just gifted that way. "I'll put the stuff together for him, no problem."

"All right, then," Castillo said, looking anxious to return to his own workload. "My condolences on your loss, Frank. Have a safe trip."

"Yeah," he said. "Thanks."

* * * *

If Frank had been asked to rate his coping skills, he probably would have given himself reasonable marks. He would figure that he met whatever life threw at him with a fair amount of equanimity, but there were several things he especially disliked and with which he did *not* necessarily cope all that well. One of these was flying. He avoided it whenever possible, but in this case, it was unavoidable. With one stopover, he wound up spending over four hours in a cramped airline seat between two portly seat mates before finally and mercifully deplaning.

Frank normally did like to drive. Driving offered a time he could use to let his mind work out problems, mull over cases and look for new solutions. Often he would suddenly realize he had been driving on "automatic pilot" for long periods of time while he had gotten lost in his labyrinths of thought.

He had about a two hour drive in his rental car from the airport to his final destination, but found he really had nothing to mull over at the moment. Surprisingly he found himself bored and uncomfortable as he drove.

This entire trip, he anticipated, was going to be uncomfortable.

The Interstate highway would only take him so far before he had to exit and take local roads. Just outside of the town of Easton, he pulled into a small gas station to fill up. There were two pumps under a metal canopy in front of a garage and mini-market, with a sign that read RALPH'S AUTOMOTIVE SERVICES. Another sign declared, PLEASE DO NOT SERVE YOURSELF GAS. WAIT FOR ATTENDANT.

Frank found this rather refreshing, given that almost all the stations he encountered back home were self-service and largely automated. Even finding a live breathing cashier, much less a station attendant, was sometimes an impossible dream. Some states, he considered, had laws prohibiting self-dispensing of fuel. Maybe this was one of them.

He didn't have long to wait before a graying, weathered-looking soul in a coverall and baseball cap strolled out from the garage, wiping his hands on a rag, and approached his window. The guy nodded to Frank and said nothing.

"Regular, please," Frank said. "Fill it up." He fumbled around under the dashboard of the rental car to find the gas tank release and popped it. The guy nodded again and reached for one of the pumps.

Frank got out to stretch his legs while the gas pumped. He noted that the guy made no offer to check the oil or wipe the windshield. Those days were long, long gone.

"How far to Easton?" he asked the guy. He noted his coverall had the name RALPH stitched over the pocket.

"You're almost there. Another mile. Visiting?"

"Sort of. Come for a funeral, actually."

Ralph nodded, a strange twitchy kind of nod, knitting his bushy eyebrows. "Sorry for your loss. Hardly anybody comes this way who isn't a local."

"You do seem a little off the beaten track here. You the owner?"

Ralph nodded again. "That would be me."

"Lived here all your life?"

The man smiled at some private joke. He shook his head, again with that strange twitchiness. "Not yet." A wise guy, okay. Another person in another small town had pulled the same old joke on him not all that long ago.

A thought occurred to Frank. "Hey, I need to find some cigars for someone I'm going to see. You wouldn't happen to sell any, would you?"

"Sorry. Not something I stock. Used to love them, myself. Gave up smoking a while back." Again he shook his head and smiled at some private joke. "Best place to find decent cigars is at the gift shop in the motel in Easton. Likely you'll be staying there."

"The Sportsman? That's where I've got a reservation."

As the guy finished up pumping the gas and extracted the pump, Frank couldn't help staring at him for a long moment. There was something vaguely familiar about him but he couldn't place it. He was fairly nondescript: average height and build, maybe in his late fifties. The eyes, the mouth. The way he stood. Something.

The guy looked up at him. "Something wrong?"

Frank shook it off. "Naw, you just looked kinda familiar for a second. Couldn't be anything. You ever been West?"

Ralph shook his head. "Nope. Don't think you and I have ever had the pleasure, mister." Beneath his baseball cap, his eyes were a rather piercing clear grey. Again that little involuntary motion of his head.

"Oh, I'm sure we haven't. I've never been around here before." Frank looked at the pump and pulled out his wallet. "You take plastic?"

"Sure," Ralph said, taking a credit card from Frank. "Be right back, I'll go run this."

Frank decided to check out the convenience store, so he followed him in. He selected a candy bar and some gum and told Ralph to put it on the card as well.

"Is the Sportsman comfortable?" Frank asked, just to have something to say.

"Yep," Ralph smiled as he swiped Frank's card through the machine and keyed in the information of the transaction. "Decent restaurant, cocktail lounge. You'll be comfortable there."

"I wouldn't mind a good meal. I'm not much of a drinker these days."

"Me neither. Kind of put the plug in the jug a while back. Don't drink, don't smoke. Don't know that I'll live longer but it'll sure seem that way." Ralph handed a receipt to Frank for his signature and then exchanged the signed copy for the customer copy. "Thank you, hope you have a nice visit."

"As nice as coming for a funeral can be," muttered Frank as he turned to leave the counter.

"One thing I've learned is certain," Ralph said. "Maybe the only thing."

"I'm sorry, what's that?" Frank asked, stopping.

"Death, I mean." Ralph shrugged. "It's a constant, isn't it? For all of us?"

"I can't argue with that," Frank allowed and continued to his car.

Strange guy. A little uncomfortable. Every word seemed to be an effort coming out of him. He still couldn't figure out why he seemed familiar. Frank somehow got some mixed messages from him, simultaneously looking for conversation but pushing away. He acted laid-back and friendly, but there was that underlying nervousness, that withdrawal.

Oh well. Small town. Different mindset and all that. He hoped everyone he met here wasn't like that. It didn't help his apprehensive mood one bit. Frank started up the car and pulled back onto the road.

The Sportsman's Lodge and Inn wasn't half bad, Frank had to admit. The reception area was clean and well maintained, and he didn't mind the decor, which went heavy on wood paneling with a hunting motif: framed reproductions of hunting scenes and even two glassy-eyed stuffed deer heads. He reflected that several women he knew wouldn't have been exactly enthused with the ambience (he got why the deer heads would displease, but *why* did it seem all the women he knew hated wood paneling so much?), but after all, he wasn't exactly there for a romantic getaway. The inn was a two-story complex, the ground floor of the main building taken up by the lobby, a restaurant, a gift/ souvenir shop, and a convenience store. The woman behind the counter was outgoing and smiling as she signed Frank in, handed him his key and gave him directions to the room.

"Let me know of you have any questions, Mr. Vandegraf. Are you here to visit family?"

"In a manner of speaking," he said, taking the key. "I'm here for a funeral."

"Oh my gosh," she said. "You must mean Muriel Lansdowne."

"That would be her."

"I'm so sorry. Terrible thing. Such a nice lady, to die in such a way."

"I'm told she had an accident? Fell off a ladder, something of that nature?"

The woman nodded gravely. She was perhaps fifty, rusty brown hair sprinkled with just a touch of grey, with large earnest eyes behind rimless glasses. "Darnedest thing. Her husband came home and found her on the ground. It seems she was trying to get a birds' nest out of a gutter of their house, or some such."

"Darnedest thing," Frank agreed.

"Poor Francis. I guess you know him, right? Such a nice fellow. He was heartbroken."

"I don't really know him," Frank admitted. "I suppose I'll get to know him this week."

"So you're a relative of Muriel's? She didn't talk much about her immediate family but I thought they were mostly gone."

"We used to be married. She and I hadn't talked in some years."

"Oh. I see. Well, my condolences, I'm sorry for your loss. We all liked Muriel very much. She was a very helpful soul, always reaching out to help others."

"That sounds like her, all right." Frank smiled wanly at the woman and waved his key on its old fashioned plastic fob. "I'll go park by the room and check it out now. Thank you."

It only took him a few minutes to decide the room would be quite satisfactory and to unpack his bag. The bed seemed comfortable, the television seemed to work, and he planned to only be sleeping and killing a small amount of time here. The room was furnished in similar fashion to the lobby: wood paneling, a couple of framed hunting prints. He was disappointed there was no glassy-eyed deer head on the wall to watch over him while slept. Next he'd check out the motel shops for the cigars and then perhaps try the restaurant. He also realized he had forgotten a few toiletries; he wasn't accustomed to travel. Well, undoubtedly he could find stuff like toothpaste in the store as well. He locked up and walked back to the lobby.

The most direct route to the stores from Frank's room was to re-trace his steps and go through the lobby. The chatty woman behind the counter was already gone, replaced by a solemn looking young man reading a magazine. He looked up and smiled at Frank as the door opened and tinkled.

"Changed shifts already?" Frank asked, nodding at the young man.

"Oh, you mean Marge? She just went to take care of a customer in the gift shop. Anything I can help you with?"

"No thanks. Actually that's where I'm heading as well. I understand you have cigars there?"

"Oh sure. We're licensed to sell package goods as well, if you want. Save you a trip down the road."

"Package goods? Oh. You mean like liquor. Alcohol." Frank had heard the term but it was not in common usage in his part of the country. The young man nodded, still smiling. His expression was slightly less glazed than the deer behind him. "Not really interested, but thanks. How's your restaurant?"

"Pretty good. I think tonight's special is pork chops."

"That would be okay, but maybe I should go light. There might well be food tonight at the gathering I'm going to. I'm mostly interested in something like a sandwich to tide me over."

"Oh yeah, no problem, plenty of sandwiches and stuff like that." The glazed but happy smile never left his face as he returned his attention to the magazine.

Frank envied people who could be that happy all the time.

The store was clearly divided into two segments, the gift shop and convenience store, each with their own cashier stand. There was one lone customer in the gift store, a guy in a windbreaker, selecting a handful of cigars out of a box in a display.

"Those are a pretty good brand, I take it?" Frank asked as he walked up to the gent inspecting the smokes. The guy seemed startled and turned his head to Frank. He had a ruddy goatee and black-rimmed glasses under a large wool newsboy cap. Wiry reddish hair stuck out from underneath. He seemed momentarily surprised before finally answering.

"I like 'em," he shrugged.

"I don't know much about this stuff. Just buying a box for someone." Frank reached over and found an unopened box, briefly inspected the package, and decided it'd do. He followed the guy back to the cash register, where Marge stood waiting for them eagerly. Obviously they weren't getting too many customers at the moment.

Funny, thought Frank, now *this* guy looks familiar to me. Something about the eyes. Is this what happens when you're in a strange place a thousand miles from home? Everyone starts looking familiar to you?

The guy had already laid a few other articles on the counter: a magazine, mouthwash, aerosol shaving cream. He said, "I got these over there in the other part of the store. It's okay if I pay for these all right here, isn't it?"

"You bet," Marge smiled. "No problem at all."

He pointed to the sparse rows behind her, where a small variety of liquor bottles were shelved. "I'd also like a bottle of that bourbon there." She reached back and grabbed a fifth of an off-brand Frank had never heard of.

"Do I need to see some ID for that alcohol?" Marge asked seriously. The guy hesitated. She broke out in a laugh. "I'm just kidding, of course, Mr. Fields. You're not all that old, but surely you're over twenty-one!"

The guy instantly relaxed and shared a self-conscious laugh with her. "Yeah, it's been a while since I got proofed. I should be flattered, shouldn't I?"

Frank remembered what else he needed. He laid the box of cigars on the counter and walked through to the convenience-store side, where he easily found a tube of toothpaste and a small bottle of shampoo. By the time he returned to Marge at the counter, the other guest was already hustling out the door with a bag under his arm.

"Find everything you need, Mr. Vandegraf?"

"I think so, thanks."

"Interesting word that Mr. Fields used there, 'getting proofed.' They don't call it that around here. The kids usually refer to it as being 'carded.' I guess in Florida they use that expression." She rang up the total.

"So he's from Florida?" Frank asked absently as he dug out his wallet and extracted some bills. This lady was like the town crier, he reflected.

"Yep. Mr. Fields just arrived last night, from Ocala, Florida. He's in the room two doors over from you."

"Maybe he's here for the funeral too," Frank said, taking his change from Marge. "We might see each other tonight."

"No, I believe he's here for something else. If you're going to the funeral parlor tonight for Muriel's wake, will you be needing directions?" She bagged up Frank's purchases and handed the paper package to him.

"As a matter of fact, sure."

"The Theodore Rollins Funeral Home, straight down the main road here about a half mile and turn right on West Elm."

WEST Elm? How big was this town anyway? Whatever. He thanked her and started to leave, then he stopped and turned around again.

"Did you know Muriel very well?"

"Pretty well, I guess. Easton isn't a very big place. We all know each other. Her family's lived here for generations. I knew her parents too."

"Tell me about her."

"Well, both parents have passed on. They left her their house, that's where she and her husband live…I mean, where she *did* live. No living relatives that I know of."

Frank reflected on how often people caught themselves on referring to a recently deceased in the present tense.

"Was she happy?"

"I'm not sure what you mean, Mr. Vandegraf."

"Did she seem happy? Living here? Her life?"

"Why…yes. She was very outgoing, very sociable. She seemed to like everybody in town. She was active in all sorts of clubs and things."

"She and her husband…got along well?"

"I should say so. They seemed very happy together. He seems a very nice man."

"I'm glad to hear that."

"She was always so interested in other people. She liked playing matchmaker when she would find someone who seemed lonely. And you know, she loved to play detective." Marge smiled just a bit at that.

"Play detective? Now I'm not sure what *you* mean, Mrs.…."

"Oh, just call me Marge. She was a great fan of mysteries…books, movies, television. She would joke about anything that came up that seemed to be a mystery. We'd kid her. Remember that TV show about the police detective's wife who solved crimes, Mrs. whatever it was?"

Frank nodded.

"She loved to watch reruns of that. We'd kid her she was like that wife, or maybe like that other character who's an elderly author who stumbles over murders all the time? Anyway, we used to kid her about being like that." She waved a hand. "Of course, there was never anything like a murder around here. The only crimes around here are pretty tame. But she was always curious about people, joking about them having mysterious skeletons in their closet and things like that."

"Yes," Frank nodded. "That sounds like her all right."

"In fact she was once married to a policeman, I understand."

"That's true. She was."

"Oh my goodness. Of course. You're him, right? I mean…."

Frank smiled. "I'm the policeman."

"I feel so stupid. You told me earlier you were married to her. Of course you're the policeman. A real detective!"

"In real life," Frank offered, "being married to a detective isn't always that great, Marge. There are things that are beyond solving, I guess." He nodded his good-bye and headed out the door.

He dropped the items in his room and returned to the restaurant. A turkey sandwich and coffee filled him up adequately. There were still a few hours to kill before the service at the funeral home. He figured he'd flop out on the bed, maybe catch a nap, or watch some television. He was back in his room, sitting on the bed, removing his shoes, when the knock came at the door.

He opened it to a paunchy guy with thinning blond hair and a rather pleasant expression.

Frank looked at him expectantly. "Yes?"

"You must be Frank," the guy said, smiling tentatively.

"I must be, you're right. Let me guess. You must be the other Frank, right?"

The visitor extended his hands as if in surrender, with a shy smile. "I always heard you were some detective. But it's Francis, actually." He still looked hesitant. They had never met in person, and Frank knew they'd both be apprehensive about how awkward this meeting was going to be.

Frank stepped back into the room. "Come on in, Francis." He offered a hand and they shook. Francis's grip was firm, Frank noted. Nothing tentative there.

"I figured you'd be here, and that it might be a good idea to come over and introduce myself." He looked around self-consciously and Frank gestured him to sit down in the only chair, sitting himself back on the bed.

"Nice of you. How have you been holding up?"

Francis shrugged, looking down and distant. "About as good as I could expect, I guess. This was one hell of a shock."

"I'm sure it was. I'm sorry for your loss."

"Nice of you to come, Frank. I appreciate it."

Frank just nodded. There was an awkward silence. The two men both gazed around the room trying to think of the next thing to say. Finally Frank reached over and picked up the box of cigars he had bought and extended it to Francis.

"I remember hearing you were a lover of cigars. Muriel happened to mention it the last time we spoke, a year or two ago. I thought I'd… well, just to let you know there're no hard feelings on my part."

Francis, surprised, took the box. He just stared at it for a long moment before looking up. "Wow. This is really nice of you."

"Sorry, I didn't get to, you know, wrap it or anything."

"No no, this is great. Just great."

"I hope the brand's to your liking. I have to admit I'm kind of ignorant about them."

Francis hefted the box up and down. "Oh yeah, this is great." He shook his head. "Wow. This means a lot. You know, when I came over here, I wasn't sure how this was gonna play out."

"I understand."

"I mean, Muriel coming back here and marrying me and all…"

"No, I get it. Everything's okay, Francis. I get the impression you were really good to her and she was happy. She deserved that."

Francis looked lost in thought for another long moment. "She never said anything bad about you, you know. No blame or stuff like that."

"It just didn't work out. It's not easy being a cop's wife. We have lots of divorces in the department. Never any time for her. Always bringing home dreadful garbage. Stuff I couldn't share with her, or anybody else for that matter."

"But she loved the whole idea of being a detective," Francis smiled. "Loved the books and the TV shows."

"I know. She got me interested in them too. I still watch some of those shows, read some of those books. When I have the time. Which isn't all that often."

"She said you'd watch with her or read something she told you about so you could tell her how unrealistic it was. How police work wasn't like that."

That made Frank smile, almost laugh. "That's still why I like them. Sometimes I wish things were as easy as in those stories. It entertains me."

"Muriel really liked other people. She loved to socialize and try to help people out."

"Yeah, that sounds right. I'm glad she found a life where she could do all that. Our life was kind of stifling for her."

They talked a few more minutes, the conversation remaining stilted and jerky. Francis talked about what their life in Easton had been like. Finally Frank broached the subject of her death.

"So, what exactly happened to Muriel, anyway?"

Francis took a long moment to compose his thoughts. "It was a freak accident. I had closed up the store early. When I got home, she wasn't in the house. I went around looking for her, and…well, I found her. Outside. On the ground next to the ladder. Her neck was broken. It was awful, just awful. I ran inside and called 911 but she was…well, she was already gone." He had to pause to regain some composure. "Damnedest thing. I don't understand why she would go up on that ladder by herself. Why couldn't she have waited for me to come back?"

"Why exactly was she up there to begin with?"

"There was a bird's nest in the gutter of the roof. She had mentioned it a couple of times. That's all I can think of." Francis drooped his head and covered it with his hands for a long moment. He continued without changing the position, talking through his hands. "She had been bugging me to get it down and move it to…someplace safe. I kept putting it off."

"Francis, it wasn't your fault this happened. Even I can see that.

Don't blame yourself."

"She fell off the damned ladder. That's the explanation the paramedics from the fire department came up with. That's what the coroner said. She had gotten up on the ladder and she...just...fell... off." Frank could tell he was beginning to cry behind those hands. "Damnedest thing. Damnedest thing ever."

Frank just waited it out. There really was nothing else he could say at that point. Well, just one.

"I'm sorry, Francis. I'm really, really sorry."

Francis looked up, his eyes a bit red, and nodded, regaining his composure.

"Well, let me tell you how to get to the viewing tonight. It's over at the Rollins Funeral Home down the street."

"Yeah, Marge in the lobby told me. Did you say viewing?" Frank felt a little uneasy.

"It's closed coffin, but you know, these wakes, people still call it 'viewing hours.' There'll be some conversation about her, Father McNulty will say some prayers, stuff like that. Then there's a kind of reception, some food and stuff, conversation about Muriel. The funeral mass will be tomorrow morning at St. Dismas' Church, and then the burial. That's sort of how we do it around here. Some places, they have the get-togethers after the burial, but we're just more comfortable doing it the night before."

Frank nodded. All this ritual over death made him uncomfortable. He figured it had to do with his own experience, having seen death up close so often. He found little in the way of comfort in religious or philosophical homilies. The familiar comforting rituals of food and socializing offered him little respite. Nothing could take away the starkness and finality he witnessed on a regular basis. It had been still another wedge between Muriel and himself.

"So, I guess I'll see you over there then?" Francis asked, standing up. Frank rose and shook his hand again.

"Sure. So, about seven?"

Francis nodded. He held up the box. "And thanks again for these. I've considered giving up smoking, but...well, you know, old habits and all. And not a good week to be thinking about such things anyway."

"You're right about that. One thing at a time."

* * * *

Driving through the town of Easton, Frank estimated there might be two or three thousand people at most living there. Muriel had grown up in Easton before moving west to attend college, get a job, and meet Frank.

After the divorce it was where she had instinctively returned. Probably everybody in town had known her.

The funeral home was full. He worked his way uncomfortably through endless introductions to neighbors and friends, explaining time and again his relation to her, and listening to innumerable variations on the theme of what a lovely woman Muriel had been and what a horrible tragedy that she was taken before her time. The coffin dominated the front of the room, covered in floral arrangements. Frank noted with relief that it was indeed closed throughout the proceedings. Folding chairs had been set up in front of the tableau.

When the gathering was asked by the priest (Father McNulty, he assumed) to take seats, Frank sought out Francis and sat beside him. After a few opening remarks, the good Father asked if anyone would like to come up and say anything about the deceased. Numerous red-eyed folks did just that, attesting to Muriel Lansdowne's kindness, good nature, and generosity. One middle-aged woman who introduced herself as Grace claimed to be "Muriel's best friend in the world."

"Why, it was only a few days ago," Grace recounted, "that Muriel was trying to find a nice lady for a local gentleman she knew who seemed lonely." Numerous heads bobbed up and down in recognition. This activity had been an open secret, it would seem. "That was her: always thinking of the other person, sensitive to their needs and their discomfort."

Frank glanced over to note Francis' decidedly forced expression. Not only, it seemed, was he familiar with the details of the story but he did not share Grace's approval of Muriel's part in it. There had to be some story there. Small towns. He considered how much he wanted to get back to his urban comfort zone again.

Finally the train of well-wishers subsided and Father McNulty stood up and led the gathering in a decade of the rosary and a few other prayers, Frank following along with polite mumbles. Finally he made a few closing remarks and announced that there would be "food and fellowship" in the adjoining hall.

Everyone filed out, half solemn and half eager for the eating and talking to come. These strange customs we observe, Frank thought to himself. Let's cry, let's eat.

"I noticed your reaction to the remark about Muriel's matchmaking," Frank murmured to Francis, mostly just to break the awkwardness, as they followed the line into the hall. Francis almost laughed aloud.

"I told her it was a bad idea. She had this interest in this guy, Ralph, he owns a filling station a way down the road. You might remember that Muriel had this idea that everyone felt just the way she did, they all needed somebody in their lives."

"Sounds familiar, yeah."

"Well, my take is that Ralph just wants to be left alone. He moved here a couple, three years back, keeps to himself. I think he just wants to keep his own counsel, you know? She didn't seem to get that."

Frank nodded. "I actually met Ralph, stopped for gas. I got the impression he was a native."

"Ralph? Naw. You mean you actually got more than a handful of words out of him?"

"Come to think of it," Frank replied, "no."

A long table crammed with various cold cut meats and salads greeted them. They grabbed plates and dug in. Conversation between them ebbed. There were a few tables to sit but most people, including Frank and Francis, simply stood and ate. Several people approached to talk to Francis and offer their support, and to introduce themselves to Frank.

After a while the talk around them had grown lively. That was the idea, Frank mused, behind gatherings such as this. "Food and fellowship," as the priest had called it, lifted the mood and brought the conversation around from the desolation of loss to happier cherished memories of the departed. It seemed to work. People would go home, if not exactly happy, at least less despondent.

The gathering began to break up around ten, and Frank accompanied Francis out to the parking lot.

There was something still nagging at Frank. Ralph Watkins had looked familiar to him, but he had dismissed the idea in the belief that Ralph had spent his life in this area, so they couldn't have possibly met. Now that he knew otherwise, that Ralph had in fact originally come from somewhere else, his curiosity was piqued. "Tell me, Francis, any idea where this Ralph Watkins guy came from before he moved here?"

Francis looked reluctant to say anything, apparently in an internal debate over how to answer. Finally, stopped in front of his car, he said, "Back east. He's from somewhere in New England."

"He told you that?"

"No. Muriel figured it out. Ralph never talks about his past."

"Muriel figured it out? What does that mean exactly?"

Another long pause before answering. Francis was not sure he wanted to continue, and did so with some obvious reluctance. "Like I said, she loved to play detective. She called Ralph the 'mystery man.' She—well, she called it putting some clues together. She figured she needed to know something about him to find him just the right girl."

He shook his head. "Damn crazy woman." He said it with surprising feeling, almost vehemence. "Forgive me, Frank. I shouldn't speak of the departed that way, certainly not someone I loved as much as her."

"What exactly did she figure out about Ralph?"

"She went by the gas station one day and while Ralph was taking care of another customer, she stepped inside–you know, where his little soda store and cash register are? She saw a Boston newspaper tucked into his chair behind the counter. That's not something that's readily available around here. You have to go to some trouble to get one, maybe drive a ways to a newsstand in a bigger town like Springdale. She figured he was catching up on news from his home area."

Something was tugging at the back of Frank's brain but he couldn't figure it out. He was still working it around when he heard the sirens.

Fire engines blared by, horns and sirens screaming, lights flashing frenetically. Everyone in the parking lot froze and turned to watch.

"Must be a good one," Francis exclaimed. "Looks like the whole blamed fire department is on its way!"

TWO

The Sportsman's Grill seemed a fairly popular restaurant; there were already a number of people seated and having breakfast when he entered it. Most of them were talking animatedly and the room buzzed with the conversations.

"Always this busy for breakfast?" he asked the young waitress who presented him a cup of coffee, a menu and a warm smile.

"Sometimes. This is a little more than usual. There's a funeral this morning, someone who was well-known around here."

Frank nodded. "That is in fact why I'm here. Everybody seems pretty excited about something, is that because of the funeral?"

"No, probably the big explosion and fire last night. The word got out about that early this morning."

Frank recalled the sirens from the evening before. "Big fire, then? Anybody hurt?"

"Oh yeah. He died. The guy who owned the service station down the road."

Frank almost dropped his menu. He did spill a little of his coffee.

"Ralph Watkins, you mean?"

"Why, yes!"

"Ralph Watkins died last night?"

"It was horrible. The gas pumps went up, the whole station. They're saying it was an accident. He set it off while he was smoking."

"While he was smoking, you say?"

"That's what they're saying. Apparently Ralph...well, you wouldn't know him, right? You're not from around here?"

"That's correct, but I did meet him yesterday, in fact."

"Well, apparently Ralph got a little drunk last night and tried to light up out front of his station and there was a leak somewhere, gas spilled on the ground or something like that, and...." She opened her eyes wide. "Poor guy."

That couldn't be the right story. Frank decided she had gotten her details wrong. Rumors were like that old game called Telephone: things changed as they passed from person to person until they had transmuted entirely. He was sure he'd hear more about this as the day went on.

"So," the waitress continued, her smile returning, "ready to order or do you need a minute?"

* * * *

The small church of Saint Dismas was crowded for the service. Frank sat in the back and saw Francis in the front pew, looking drained and downcast. It was finally all hitting home for him. Frank was quite familiar with the process many loved ones went through in coming to grips with a loss—much more familiar than he had ever wanted to be.

The Mass went quickly for Frank as his mind spun throughout the service. Father McNulty offered more words in memory of the departed Muriel. Soon Frank found himself driving in the procession to the cemetery, where he joined the group congregating around the open grave. The priest said some more prayers with obvious feeling, blessed the gathering, and left the final descent of the coffin into its gaping hole to the grave tenders.

Frank had still not had the chance all morning to approach Francis, who had continued to grow more haggard and morose looking as the proceedings continued. Now Frank hoped they'd have a chance to speak before they left the cemetery grounds.

He walked across the stream of departing mourners towards Francis, who stood near the grave conversing earnestly with Father McNulty. The priest was looking down, his left ear to Francis, listening intently, and nodding at what was being said. Frank began to have second thoughts that this was the moment to talk with Francis, but when he was a few steps away and hesitated, both men looked up and smiled at him. In Francis' case the smile was wan and weak, but it seemed welcoming.

Father McNulty motioned him towards them and extended a hand. "I take it you must be Detective Vandegraf," he said. "It was good of you to come. I've heard a few things about you." He was perhaps fifty, with a spark of merry intelligence in his eyes, and a deep voice tinged with a melodic Irish brogue.

"I hesitate to ask what those things might be," Frank said, taking the priest's hand. "Please, call me Frank, Father."

"Kieran McNulty," the priest replied, his smile growing. "And I'd be pleased to have you call me simply Kieran, Frank. Take my word, the reputation that precedes you is admirable."

"I can only hope that's the truth."

"Believe me, neither Muriel nor Francis ever had an unkind word for you, lad." He shrugged. "The past is the past." His grip was quite firm. Frank wondered if the good Father had once been a prizefighter or a longshoreman.

Francis continued to make an effort at smiling but it was obvious it was a fight. Frank turned to him and said, "Sorry I didn't get the chance to speak with you at the service. How are you doing?"

"I guess everything hit me particularly hard last night," he replied. "Maybe we can talk a little later. Will you be heading home soon or will we have a chance?"

"My flight's a redeye tonight. We can talk before then."

Francis nodded.

"By the way," Frank continued, "I heard about the fire last night. Someone said it was Ralph Watkins, is that right?"

McNulty nodded gravely. He was still holding Frank's hand in his. "A horrible thing."

"The story I got was that he drank too much and tried to light a cigarette around his pumps. That can't be right."

Finally letting go of Frank's hand, McNulty stared at him as he continued to nod. "That is indeed the story I heard as well. Except it was a cigar, not a cigarette."

"Something about that seems strange," Frank said.

"Ralph was quite the cigar smoker," Francis said hesitantly. "And he used to be seen in the local bar all the time. Maybe it's not so strange." He turned to McNulty and extended his own hand to shake. "Thanks, Father, we'll talk later then?"

"Of course. Give me a call later on and we'll talk as we arranged."

"Frank, forgive me, I gotta run." He shook Frank's hand as well.

"Sure, Francis. I'll give you a call before I leave, or why don't you just come by the motel when you're free, okay? We really should talk before I leave."

As Francis trudged away across the rolling grass of the cemetery, McNulty turned to Frank and his face grew more serious. "Just what did you mean, that something seems strange?"

"Well, I didn't know this guy Ralph, of course, but I spoke with him when I stopped at his station on the way in yesterday. He told me he had given up smoking and drinking."

McNulty nodded more vigorously. He paused a moment as if judging whether to go on and then said, "I have to tell you, it struck me a bit odd as well. Can I confide something in you, relying upon your professional ethics as a police investigator, perhaps?"

"You're not going to divulge a confessional admission or anything like that?"

McNulty laughed. "Oh, Lord no. That's a sacred bond, lad. The seal of the confessional is sacrosanct. Not to mention, the man was not a churchgoer, much less to my church. No, but this has to do with a different kind of confidentiality. You see, Ralph and I shared a certain fellowship. Both of us had put the plug in the jug some while back."

"He used that exact expression," Frank said.

"We're both recovering alcoholics. Often were the times one of us would call the other for a bit of moral support in a rugged moment."

"A twelve-step program?" Frank asked.

"An anonymous one, and we can only 'out' ourselves and not others; but with death that no longer applies." He read Frank's expression. "What, you think men of the cloth aren't susceptible to such maladies, now?"

"No, I don't think that one bit," replied Frank. "Not much surprises me, Padre. Not anymore."

"Kieran, please. That Father stuff is appropriate in some cases but not here, all right now, are we agreed? At any rate, I didn't know all that much about Ralph but I did know that after he moved here, he made the effort to clean up his life, and to my knowledge, the man had not touched a drop in at least a year. And as for the cigars—it was my understanding he had indeed given up smoking as well."

"I suppose people do relapse."

"Of course. Of course. But, Frank, I must tell you, it doesn't feel right in Ralph's case. Do you know the feeling when your gut just tells you something isn't right?"

"Oh, do I. I couldn't do my job if I didn't have that particular sense."

"Well then, just between you and me, lad, the story doesn't feel right, and I am strongly inclined to the opinion there is more to this than I've heard so far."

"Is it possible that you and I have heard twisted rumors? That the real story is something different?"

"I'd like to believe that, but the unfortunate truth is that I got the story from two of my parishioners, who happen to be a captain of the Fire Department and a dispatcher from the local Sheriff's Department. When they found Ralph's terribly burned body—and may he rest in eternal peace—there was part of a whiskey bottle beside him and there were shards of a cigar and a burned remain of a matchbook nearby as well. It was a foregone conclusion. Or so it would seem."

"Are you saying you suspect that it wasn't an accident? That maybe this was all set up to look like it?"

McNulty extended his lower lip and looked thoughtful. "Foul play? A bit dramatic. We're not in a television melodrama or a turgid whodunit book, are we now? Or back in your big bad city teeming with ill will?" At this he smiled again and winked mischievously.

"Still. You agree it's strange. Something isn't adding up here, is it?"

"Agreed. Perhaps it was an accident of a different sort."

"What do you know about Ralph Watkins anyway? I was told he only moved here a few years ago? That he kept to himself?"

"A closed book, that one. Wasn't of the tendency to let people in very close. He moved here about—oh, I'd say two, three years ago. Took over the station, which had been closed for some time, and got it running again. He was a good mechanic and ran a pretty decent business."

"He didn't socialize much, I gather."

"No, not at all. He was cordial enough to everybody, if a bit awkward. Struck me as above-average intelligent as well."

"You seem to have gotten to know him?"

"Perhaps a bit more than others, once he started coming to our meetings. We'd have coffee together afterward now and then. He was awkward, as I said—uncomfortable with opening up. We discussed feelings and such now and then, for what they were worth. It was a slow process and still in progress."

Despite himself, Frank felt the gears of his investigating mind kick in. Before he realized it he found himself jumping into the hunt. "He wasn't the only mechanic in town, was he?"

"Oh no. There are two other mechanics around Easton. One runs another gas station, on the other end of town. The other just fixes cars and such."

"Might there have been a business rivalry, that sort of thing?"

McNulty waved the idea off with his hand. "You're suggesting one of the other mechanics in town eliminated him? No, no. Both are decent lads I've known for many years now. And it's not as if any of them are hurting for business either. Everybody's got a car or a truck or one of each and there's plenty of business to go around. It's hardly a cutthroat industry in these parts. Back in your big city, do mechanics go around eradicating one another in a violent manner?"

"More likely they're non-violently overcharging their customers," Frank replied. "You said you spoke to someone at the Sheriff's. How are the local police regarding this, as an accident?"

"It would seem, yes."

"I'm thinking perhaps I need to go talk to them, just air my misgivings before I leave. Do you feel strongly enough about it to do the same with me?"

McNulty considered that. "I'm not sure, Frank. Let me think on that a bit. For now, it's just strange to me. I don't necessarily suspect foul play afoot or anything like that. But by all means, follow your own conscience on how you wish to proceed."

The twinkle in McNulty's eye clued Frank that perhaps he wasn't as much the small-town cleric as he was enjoying playing the role of one. Frank asked directions to the Sheriff's station and they chatted a bit further before shaking hands and bidding one another goodbye.

* * * *

The Freeman County Sheriff's Department was a long, low building with a decent-sized parking lot. Double glass doors led into the station. A uniformed receptionist watched him approach as she sat at a gap in a glass wall at a high counter. Before he was halfway to her, she said, "Can I help you?"

Frank decided it wouldn't hurt to display his ID and badge and had it out at the ready. She gave him a polite smile as she looked it over.

"I was wondering if I could speak to whoever is dealing with last night's death of Ralph Watkins," he said.

"The Sheriff's unavailable at the moment but you can speak with

Deputy Maravich," she said, staring blankly at him, vestiges of the polite but blank smile refusing to leave her face.

"That sounds like a good place to start," Frank said. "Thank you."

She punched a number on her desk phone and spoke into her headset: "There's a Detective Vanderbilt from out of town to see you about the Ralph Watkins accident. Okay, I'll tell him."

Then she pointed to the seats along the far wall of the reception area. "He'll be right out. Please take a seat, Detective Vanderbilt."

"That's Vandegraf, actually," Frank said. "Thanks."

He strolled across the room to the benches and sat down, gazing around at the surroundings. This couldn't be more different from the police station to which he was accustomed. It was quiet, modern, spacious, and nearly empty.

A tall, dark-haired, serious-looking uniformed man emerged from around a corner. "Detective Vanderbilt?"

Frank hoisted himself to his feet again. "That's Vandegraf. Frank Vandegraf."

The deputy extended a hand. "I'm Deputy Sheriff Lee Maravich. Nice to meet you. Why don't you come on back?" Frank detected a bit of a drawl.

Frank followed the deputy back around the same corner, down a corridor and into a large room that was divided up into about a dozen cubicles. Now Frank could hear familiar sounds: phones ringing, computer noises, the murmur of voices. Maravich stepped into one of the cubicles and motioned for Frank to take one of the seats facing the desk.

Once they were both seated, Frank went through the ritual again of showing his badge and credentials and briefly explained his reason for being there. Maravich said, "So you're here about Ralph Watkins too, huh? Must be something going on with that whole thing."

"Excuse me?" Frank asked.

"The Sheriff is in with two somber sorts right now, also from out of town," Maravich said. "What, are you guys coming in on buses to talk about Ralph?"

"I've got nothing to do with them," Frank said, extending his hands.

Maravich sat back in his swivel chair. "So what specifically brings you here anyway?"

Frank explained why he had come to Easton in the first place and gave a bit of his own background, then laid out the misgivings he harbored about the story he had heard behind the death of Ralph Watkins. Maravich listened carefully, an earnest expression on his face.

"I realize I don't know that much about the man," Frank summed up his explanation, "but there's something that just didn't ring true to me about this. I figured it couldn't hurt to come forward and just tell you about my conversation with Watkins yesterday. I might possibly have been the last person to speak with him while he was still alive."

Maravich nodded and seemed lost in thought for several seconds. "So Ralph told you he had given up drinking and smoking."

"That's right."

"You have to admit, that's not an awful lot to go off of, sir. Even if he did say that, people do say things that might not be true. Maybe he wanted people to *think* he had stopped drinking and smoking, if you get my meaning?"

"That's not out of the question," Frank allowed. "But it was odd that he would bring it up to me. I was a stranger, passing through. Why mention it at all? Why bother convincing me either way? Why would he even care what I thought?"

Maravich shrugged. "It is odd, I'll give you that."

"All I'm saying is that maybe he didn't just get drunk and set his station on fire. I'm just a visitor here, I'm leaving for home tonight, and of course it's your case. I just wanted to have my observations on the record, for you to be able to consider that."

"And I appreciate that, Detective…Vandegraf?" Frank nodded. "I'm sorry for your loss. I've known Francis and Muriel for a while now. She was a very nice lady."

Frank took out one of his business cards and handed it to the deputy. "I'm at the Sportsman Lodge if you need to reach me today, and my cell phone is on my card. I'm heading back tonight."

Maravich's phone buzzed and he picked up the receiver, muttering a few terse "Uh-huhs" and hanging up. "Forgive me, we have a situation I have to move on right away." He rose and shook Frank's hand, looking suddenly hurried.

"I understand, Deputy Maravich. Thanks for your time. I can find my way out."

"Appreciate that. Have a safe journey home. Oh, by the way?"

"Yes, Deputy?"

"I place you now. Once or twice Muriel mentioned you in passing. That she had previously been married to a police detective."

"Huh. I hope it wasn't all bad."

"As a matter of fact, I do not recall anything bad. She was almost proud of you, I got the impression once."

Frank shrugged. How about that.

In the lobby on his way out, Frank noted a heavy-set uniformed man that he figured was the Sheriff, talking earnestly with a man and a woman in buttoned-up dark suits. They seemed out of place here. To Frank they looked a lot like Federal agents he had known. It looked as if this was quite the busy place today. All three, with solemn expressions, shot him a glance as he passed.

Check-out time was still a couple of hours away but Frank figured he'd pack up and spend the time with Francis before the drive back to the airport for his late flight home. Francis did not answer his phone so he left a message when voice mail cut in. Frank figured Francis had met up with the priest as they had been discussing earlier. Apparently everything had finally hit Francis emotionally and he was in need of some spiritual and emotional support. He hoped they'd have the chance to have another conversation before he had to depart.

He quickly packed and stretched out on the bed to watch television to bide a little time. Evidently he was still tired or the bed was inordinately comfortable; he drifted off and suddenly found himself being roused from his catnap by a knocking on his door.

"Deputy Maravich. Fancy seeing you here."

"Detective Vandegraf. Got a minute for a few words?"

"Sure, come on in. Don't tell me you already decided to pursue the question of Ralph Watkins further?"

"Actually, no," Maravich said as he stepped into the room. Frank motioned him to the lone chair where Francis Lansdowne had sat the evening before. "The Sheriff seems satisfied that it was an accident. This is in fact a different matter. Marge Palmer up at the front tells me you had a conversation with another guest here last night, a Barry Fields?"

"Barry, that's his first name?" The lyrics "Straw Barry Fields Forever" suddenly started playing in his brain. "I wouldn't call it a conversation. We exchanged some brief words in the gift shop. He wasn't a very talkative fellow."

Maravich nodded. He pulled out a smart phone and keyed up a photo. "Would this be the man you spoke with last night?"

Frank looked at a close-in shot of a man's face. He was very familiar with this kind of photo. He took them often himself.

"This man is dead. You took this at the scene of the death?"

Maravich nodded. His hand shook slightly as he held up the phone. Frank took the phone from him and looked more closely.

"This was your 'situation' a while ago, I take it."

"Is he the man you spoke with last night?" Maravich repeated, looking concerned.

Frank stared at the photo silently for a long moment. "He's different. Last night he had a beard, a goatee rather." He made a gesture around his mouth with his fingers. "And he had glasses. His hair was ruddier. But...yes. The facial structure is right. I'd say this is the same guy." He handed the phone back to the deputy. "What happened?"

"He was found dead in his car on the highway about ten miles away. Somebody shot him."

"You gotta be kidding!"

"No, sir, I am not. Looks as if he was driving out of town early this morning, maybe around four. He was shot in the head, after which his car drove into the piling of an overpass."

Frank shook his head. This was as insane as anything he had to regularly deal with back home.

"You're sure it's the same man?" Maravich asked again.

Frank nodded. "Pretty sure. The nose, the eyebrows. The physiognomy of the face. His hair looks to be a different color but it's the same texture."

Maravich smiled ruefully. "Sounds like you're good police, as they say. Marge couldn't make a definite ID. She thought it wasn't the same guy."

"No, it's the same guy, but he clearly went to some effort to change his appearance all of a sudden." Something began to stir in the back of his mind. "He had identification, I suppose? And he must have had something to bring you back here—a receipt from the motel?"

The deputy nodded. "He had a Florida driver's license and a credit card in the name of Barry Fields. His receipt from the Sportsman was in his pocket."

"He was leaving town in the dead of night," Frank murmured, searching his brain. What was bugging him? There was something...

"He must have flown in; the car was a rental from the airport, we learned that already. But it looks like he wasn't planning on flying out again. He was heading in the wrong direction, for one thing, and we haven't found plane tickets or anything like that yet. Maybe he was going to drive home to...I think it's Ocala?"

A sudden connection virtually exploded in Frank's head all at once. He thought he remembered why the guy had looked familiar. He wasn't positive but...

"I don't think his real name is Barry Fields," Frank said. "And I don't think he was really from Florida."

"What are you saying, Detective?"

"If what I suspect is true, this guy's name is Artie." He spent another few seconds lost in thought. "Artie Burns. At least that's the name I know him by."

"Artie Burns." Maravich stared at Frank. "Who's that and why do you think that?"

"It's the look in his eyes when we talked. It just hit me this instant, why I was so sure he looked familiar. Back home, we once picked him up on suspicion. Questioned him and had to let him go when he lawyered up."

Maravich's eyebrows raised. This must be like listening to a fairy tale for him, Frank figured.

"Burns was—I guess you'd call him a fixer. He would travel around to look after the interests of the organization back East. Clean up messes. Or so we believed."

"You mean, he was like a hit man," Maravich said.

"He was a person of interest in a suspicious death. The victim was a local businessman we suspected of various criminal activities; he might have run afoul of some out of town interests. We don't like wise guys in our city to begin with but we *really* don't like it when carpetbaggers come in to get a foot in the door and do things like murders for hire. We found this guy about to head to the airport. I was one of two detectives who questioned him. He claimed he was a salesman making the rounds, and then all of a sudden this slick expensive lawyer showed up and popped him. His story stunk to us, but we couldn't hold him."

Maravich was rapt at the story. He nodded thoughtfully. "And you think this Barry Fields is the same guy, this Artie Burns? Why?"

"Like I said. It's the eyes. Mostly he looked different from this guy. His hair was different, he had no eyeglasses, and he had, like, this bushy mustache but otherwise he was clean-shaven. But the eyes, they were the same. I was sitting across the table from him. The conversation wasn't all that long. He didn't talk much. But he would stare at us. Cold. Sizing us up every second, figuring his angle. We call it bad intent. Kind of unsettling, like a snake looking at a bird? When the guy you call Fields looked at me in the gift shop, I flashed on that stare, that look. It took me a while to place it, to put the circumstances and the name to it."

"You were sure this guy Burns was the killer in your case?"

"We had that strong feeling. You probably know what I'm talking about." Maravich nodded slowly. "The death was made to look like an accident. The victim fell out of a window at a construction site late at night. It didn't make sense. And then this Burns guy turned up. He'd been in town for a day or two before the death and he was leaving immediately afterward. Really fishy. But we didn't have enough to hold him."

"And you never cleared the case, am I right?"

Frank shook his head. "We already had our eyes on the victim before he turned up dead. Not worth going into details here, but he was deep into all sorts of stuff. We were sure it was an arranged death. But we could never prove it."

"How long ago was this?"

"Two and a half years ago."

Maravich nodded again. "We don't get a lot of investigations we can't close, but there have been a couple I was personally involved with, and I know how they particularly rankle."

Frank returned his knowing nod. The deputy considered all this further before continuing. "If you're right about this, then we've got some kind of organized crime thing here? That staggers the imagination, I've got to say. Why was the guy here, and how and why did he get killed? If this is at all possible, I'm totally at sea."

"I'd like to be of some help to you here. I don't want to get in the way where I'm not wanted or anything, but..."

"I understand, Detective. In fact I wish you could hang around another day or two, be some help as a witness and a background source." He stared at Frank for a long moment.

"I think I might be able to arrange that," Frank said. "Long as you're sure I'm welcome."

* * * *

"Frank, this is a surprise to hear from you. You're not back already?"

"Nope, I'm still in Easton. Lieutenant, I'm going to need to stay here for a little longer than I originally anticipated. Any problem with my taking a few more days?"

"Frank, you've got ridiculous amounts of time accrued, we both know that. What do you want me to tell you? Part of me could really use you back. Part of me is delighted to see you're finally taking some time off away from work, relaxing for a change."

"Relaxing…yeah. Anyway, you're okay with that?"

"Sure. How long are you thinking?"

"I'm thinking staying over this weekend. The earliest return flight I can get is Sunday—be back at work Monday?"

"I do think the unit can survive without you for a few more days, Frank. I would have expected you to take the weekend at very least anyway. Come back Tuesday." Castillo paused a moment in thought. "Frank, I know you weren't all that close with your ex any more, but if you need some time for closure or whatever that you didn't anticipate, feel free to take whatever you need. As I said, you have it coming."

Frank was about to tell him that wasn't the case, but thought better of it. The less said the better. In any case, he was touched by Castillo's unexpected show of support. "Thanks, Lou. I should be fine coming back Tuesday."

"Morrison won't be happy to have to carry your cases a few more days, but he'll survive."

Chances are Marlon Morrison wasn't doing any work on them anyway, Frank considered. He thought better of saying that as well.

* * * *

Maravich had been spending the time trying to hunt down anyone else at the lodge who might have encountered the mysterious

Barry Fields. Frank located the deputy in the lobby, talking and vigorously taking notes. Marge was behind the counter with the young clerk Frank had encountered the day before. One of the housekeepers was also standing nearby, looking nervous. Clearly the news of the death of their guest had upset them all, but also aroused their curiosity and sense of excitement.

"Okay, I was able to switch my flight to late Sunday. Now as long as I can extend my stay here, I'm available all weekend."

Marge forced a brave smile. "It should be no problem, Mr. Vandegraf. Your room is still available for...how long, until Sunday, you say?"

"Yes, thank you, that would be great."

She reached under the counter and pulled out a new registration form and a pen. "Goodness, this is just horrible. That poor man. How could such a thing have happened?"

"That's what we'll find out, Marge," Maravich said, closing his notebook. "Thank you all for your help."

He turned to shake hands with Frank. "You available a little later today, Detective? Maybe a couple hours, so I can gather my facts together and prepare the Sheriff for you?"

He made a wry grin. Frank surmised that the Sheriff was not going to be as happy about his involvement as Maravich seemed to be.

"Sure. I'll give you a call before I come by."

"See you then."

Back in his room, Frank tried calling Francis once again. He got his voice mail again. Apparently the Padre's counseling services were being taken good advantage of.

"Francis, it's Frank. My plans have changed a bit and I'll be here until Sunday. I'd still love to have dinner with you tonight, and maybe spend a little time with you Saturday as well. Give me a call back when you get this."

Frank had to wonder why he was going to such lengths to be friendly to Francis, a man he had never met before yesterday and who had married his ex-wife. He decided there was something there he needed to work out over time. Guilt, maybe? Regret?

He had never blamed Muriel for ending their marriage. When all was said and done, he was a lousy husband. He knew he was prone to distraction and self-absorption, perhaps not always being "emotionally available," as the TV shrinks liked to say. Being a cop, especially one "also married to his job," as she had put it often, just compounded it. He had always wished her well. He was sure he was genuinely pleased to discover that she had been happy here in Easton with Francis.

But for whatever reason, he felt some imperative to be nice to Francis. And right now the man sure seemed to need it. He had looked terrible this morning at the service and the burial. In any case it felt like the right way to go.

It didn't take long for Francis to return his call. "Frank, I need to take care of a few more things but I'd love to meet up for dinner. How about around seven, that work for you?"

That would give him a couple of hours to spend at the Sheriff's. "That'd be fine. Where's a good place to meet?"

"Why don't you come over here? I'm not a great chef but I can thaw out a couple of steaks and barbecue them up, add some trimmings and stuff."

"Are you sure that's okay? Do you really feel up to it? And, well… not gonna feel a little strange, having me in your home right now?"

"Frank, I think I'd welcome that. I could use having something to do to keep me busy today. You and I can talk about Muriel and fill each other in. I think we're both okay with that, aren't we?"

"I certainly am. If you're positive?"

"Positive."

"Seven then. Can I bring a bottle of wine? I'm not a big drinker, but maybe this calls for it."

"Works for me. See you then."

He returned to the gift shop and found a reasonable looking bottle of red wine. Marge Palmer was once again behind the counter.

"What a couple of days," she remarked as she rang up his purchase.

"Tell me about it. Is it always this exciting around here?"

"My gosh, no! I've never seen a week like this one! First Muriel's crazy accident, then Ralph's horrible accident, and now that strange man getting shot. Do you remember much about him?"

Frank cast his eyes around the shop and replayed the short events of the previous day. "As I told the Deputy, we must have exchanged half a dozen words with each other. I asked him about the cigars he was buying. That was about it. Then I heard your discussion with him here at the counter while he was paying for the stuff he bought." He recreated the scene of the counter in his mind. Cigars. Shaving cream. Mouthwash. "He asked you for a bottle of bourbon, didn't he?"

"Why, that's right. A fifth of Rebel Jim. We only carry a couple of brands, so I remember that."

"He joked about getting ID checked for that."

"Yes, he used an odd word. 'Proofed,' did he say?"

"People say that on the East Coast a lot. Kids say that. Might be he was from there."

He bought cigars. Only two. Was that worth noting?

Frank thought about the eyeglasses. Heavy, dark-rimmed. In his mind's eye he tried to conjure up the moment again. What was it...

The guy's eyes. The glasses didn't distort them. They were a pretty mild prescription.

Or they were just glass. Fakes. Props.

"Did you talk to him much while he was here at the inn?" Frank asked her.

"No, we spoke briefly when he checked in, the usual stuff. He wasn't into small talk. He wasn't rude or anything, just...reticent."

He bought shaving cream. He knew he was going to shave off his goatee.

He bought mouthwash. Well...okay, not everything had to be meaningful, Frank decided. Maybe for after the bourbon.

"When did he check in?"

"Let's see, you arrived here yesterday, that was Thursday. He checked in Wednesday night."

"Did he have a reservation?"

"No. We had plenty of vacancies. He said he didn't need anything fancy, just a simple single."

"Forgive me, I'm just curious, if you don't mind telling me any of this. Did he happen to mention why he was staying here in Easton for a couple of nights?"

"Oh sure. I guess he was one of the people who had started up an internet retail site of some kind down in Florida. They were starting to grow and he was scouting out possible locations...I guess where they could set up warehouses, distribution outlets. He said they wanted to find centrally located places where there was a lot of land available at a reasonable price. I gathered he was going to use this as a base of operations and drive around all day yesterday. He even left me a business card. I gave it to the Deputy."

"And I assume he showed you, what, a driver's license?"

"Yes, he was from Ocala, Florida. "

"And he paid with a credit card, right?"

"Yes, that's right."

"And he checked out really early."

"Yes. I wasn't on the desk. It was a couple of hours after midnight. Julius was on duty. Mr. Fields came in, said he got an urgent business call and had to leave, and settled his bill."

"And I assume Deputy Maravich asked you all that," Frank smiled. "I'm not trying to play policeman here or anything. As I said, just curious, like you are. Strange guy, you're right."

"He apparently made another joke too. Julius said he made a joke about being the company's go-to guy and having to put out some more fires."

THREE

Back in his room he decided enough time had passed and he called Maravich, who told him to give him another half hour and then he could come by the station at his convenience. Frank was there in thirty-five minutes.

He was escorted to a small but comfortable conference room. He couldn't help but compare its well-kept cleanliness to the bare-bones-functional rooms of his own unit back home.

Maravich sat at a table with the stocky uniformed man Frank had seen earlier. The man rose and extended his hand. "You must be Detective Vandegraf, right?"

"Frank Vandegraf. You can call me Frank."

"Sheriff Rick Riculla, Frank." His bushy mustache and matching eyebrows were iron gray. The man seemed friendly enough but reserved. "Lee's filled me in on who you are and why you are in town. My deepest condolences on your loss. Muriel Lansdowne was a terrific lady."

Frank nodded acknowledgment.

"Now. Having said that, I appreciate your coming in to confer with us like this, but I'd be less than honest if I didn't tell you up front I do not share my deputy's enthusiasm for it. If it weren't for the fact that Lee Maravich is one hell of a lawman who commands my personal respect as much as any man on this force, I would have in fact overruled his invitation to you, hands down. Nothing personal, I hope you can understand where this is coming from."

There was an awkward moment of silence among the three. Maravich, sitting back with arms crossed and eyebrows raised, glanced back and forth between the two men to see what would ensue.

Frank rubbed the back of his neck with his hand and sighed.

"No, I understand, Sheriff. I do not take it personally. Earlier today I told Deputy Maravich that in my own department, we do not appreciate carpetbaggers. I don't think any cop anywhere does. But that's not why I'm here. I want to make it clear I didn't come here to intrude on your investigation or to step into it in any way. I came forth as a witness who spoke with your victim, and to provide background information that may hopefully be of value to your department's investigations. Nothing else. Promise."

Riculla chewed on that for a long moment—almost literally, it seemed to Frank, as his jaw moved under that walrus mustache. Finally he gave a terse nod and directed a piercing stare at his visitor.

"All right. I hope that what you've got to offer helps us. I'll leave you two to talk." He patted Maravich on the shoulder. "Got a situation that needs my attention. Lee will bring me up to speed later."

He nodded again, shook Frank's hand once again, and left the cubicle.

Maravich gestured for Frank to have a seat and reached for a ceramic mug on the table next to his notepad. "I'm getting a refill on my coffee. Can I bring you one? "

"Sure. It's gotta be better than the coffee back at my station house."

"Probably," Maravich smiled, rising. "Though likely not much better. Black okay?"

"Black's great," said Frank. "Thanks."

Maravich had pegged the coffee right, even referring to it as "universal cop coffee" while handing Frank his own mug. Frank wasn't picky; it would do just fine.

"How's the investigation going?"

"Lots more has become known already. Our guy was shot in the head with a .22."

"A twenty-two, you say?"

Maravich nodded. "It did the job. Looks like it was a rifle. There are two overpasses along that stretch of the road, a couple hundred feet or so apart. It looks as if the shooter was on or near one overpass and plugged him as he went by. Hit him in the side of the head near the neck. He lost control of the car and must have been doing a good clip, because his momentum carried him pretty forcefully into the piling of the second overpass. The coroner's preliminary report indicates he probably was dead right then."

"Sounds like a pretty good shot," Frank mused. "Car going by at, what, fifty or sixty maybe?"

"That sounds about right."

"One shot, right?"

"Right. Only one bullet in the victim."

"So the shooter was lying in wait for him, and must have known he was coming."

"Sure seems that way. But maybe he wasn't as good as all that. There was only one bullet in the victim, but so far two more bullets have been found near the first overpass. One lodged in a tree by the side of the road."

Frank digested that. "Could there have been more than one shooter? Did the bullets all seem to come from the same source?"

"Not totally out of the question. We're still working on the ballistics and such, but so far it's consistent with one shooter only. There were some footprints and what looked like a knee print on the embankment alongside the first overpass. Our guys are still out there going over the site."

"What's that stretch of road like along there?"

"It feeds into the Interstate about ten or fifteen miles further down the road. Well-traveled during the day, but fairly desolate. Farms, road stands, a gas station or two. No lights, just reflectors along the roadside. A divided county road crosses it and it used to be a grade crossing. After a number of accidents the state finally built overpasses about ten years back."

"So…dark, desolate. A perfect place for an ambush. *If* you knew your man was going to be coming through there in the dead of the night."

Maravich nodded. "I would say so."

"I'm curious, if I may ask, what else did you find in his car?"

"Not much. The only thing in the glove compartment was his rental agreement. He picked up the car at the airport Wednesday evening and had an open-end return with an estimation of four days. The return location said New York City."

"So he was planning on driving across country, it would seem. Was he carrying a weapon?"

"Nope. No gun. He had a multi-tool knife, like a Swiss Army knife kind of thing, in his bag. You know, with blades, screwdrivers, picks…"

Frank nodded. "Sure. Everything imaginable. Scalpel, pitchfork, microwave oven, shortwave radio…"

Maravich blinked then laughed.

"He was traveling light. Small bag. He had only a couple changes of clothes, socks, underwear, all that stuff. A few hygiene articles like a toothbrush. Looked as if he jammed it all in pretty quickly. There was also a small package of business cards, the same kind he gave to Marge at the lodge."

"Phone?"

"Yeah. One of those month-to-month cell phones. Like he had picked it up in a hurry somewhere."

"How about the glasses? Did he have them?"

"As a matter of fact, yes. They were under the seat of the car."

"Have you had a chance to inspect them? I have a hunch they were props, just clear glass."

Maravich said they had not done so yet. Frank recounted his recollections of the man's appearance. Maravich began to jot notes down on his legal pad.

"So let's go over this in as much detail as you can, Frank. Why exactly did you have suspicions about this Barry Fields?"

Frank recounted their brief conversation over the cigars. He mentioned the joke he had made about being "proofed."

"Okay, so that led you to believe he was from somewhere on the East Coast. But his license did say he was from Florida. And his business cards were from a Florida company."

"He just struck me as more northeastern seaboard, New York or New England. Not that there aren't a lot of transplants to Florida. But my definite impression was he was at least originally from further north than Florida."

Maravich asked more questions, prompting Frank to fill in all the details he could remember. The deputy took copious notes, stopping him to clarify points, ask questions and direct the topic along some related avenue. Frank found himself impressed with the man's careful thoroughness. He was beginning to suspect that he would have been a good cop no matter where he lived, someone who would have been a valuable asset in Frank's own Personal Crimes unit.

"Now tell me some more about this Artie Burns guy you think is one and the same person as Barry Fields."

Frank nodded. "I can't be sure that was his real name either. His ID was in that name. He said he was an insurance salesman from Waukegan. He was allegedly passing through town to do a check-in on some contacts. Before we could press him for corroboration of those contacts, his attorney had shown up and was shutting down our interrogation."

"And from the git-go you weren't buying it. Why did you pick him up to begin with?"

"Let me back up and tell you about the case we were investigating. It was a guy named Lon Shumer. A real piece of work. We were pretty sure he had his hand in all sorts of things: drugs, numbers, prostitution, you name it. His public face was that he owned a couple of large construction firms and some other ancillary enterprises. He was smart, I'll give him that. He was a skillful money launderer and he had, like, a battalion of sharp lawyers. We had been after him for years, waiting for him or one of his people to slip up, make some mistake. Someone always does."

Maravich nodded. "We don't like to make mistakes, but we get to make a few and we're still in the game. Lawbreakers only get to make one."

"Exactly. That's one of the few advantages we have on our side. So it was a waiting game on our part. Word came in that Shumer was involved in some kind of labor dispute and that it was getting tense. Worse for him, as it turns out, there were some feelers coming through to us from intermediaries that he might be willing to make some kind of deal."

"A deal with the police you mean?"

"Yeah. Nothing specific had been established but a couple people from the District Attorney's office came around, floating ideas with us and some of the other units, figuring out what kinds of things might be on the table. They didn't mention Shumer by name but, from the questions they were asking, it was pretty clear to us he was one of the guys they had in mind. We didn't like the idea of him getting any kind of a deal and skating on anything, but it wasn't going to be our call."

Maravich nodded again. He had stopped writing, caught up in the story Frank was recounting.

"Then late one evening, Shumer took a dive off a building his company was putting up. The crew coming in early the next morning found him in the debris. There didn't seem to be any witnesses but we located a couple of associates who said they had been drinking with Lon the night before and he had started complaining about the cutbacks and shoddy work that was being done on his building and how he was going to start kicking some butts."

"And next thing you know, he somehow finds his way up on his building and tumbles off."

"There you go. Nothing at all suspicious about that, right?"

Maravich smiled grimly, eyebrows raised, and shook his head.

"So how did this Burns character fit into this scenario? How did you come to suspect him?"

"It was part footwork and part dumb luck. As I said, we smelled a rat. His 'friends' who were telling us about the drinking, they were a little sketchy to us, too. We were checking security cameras around the site for that night and found a photo of the guy making a transaction at a nearby ATM. We lucked out on a canvas of nearby hotels. He was staying at a hotel about six blocks away. And he was checking out when we got there."

"Seems like if he was the fixer you thought, he would have been long gone. What was this, a day or two later?"

"Almost twenty-four hours later. Another piece of luck on our part, a major storm somewhere in the Midwest. His flight had been cancelled. He couldn't re-book until the weather cleared, and those flights were stacked up."

"Where was he flying to? You said he claimed to be from Waukegan, that's near Chicago."

"His flight was to Chicago, but here's the thing, we found out he also had a connector on to Boston."

"Hmm. So you picked this guy up and brought him in for questioning?"

"Right. That's when we got the story. His ID said he was Arthur Burns. He said he went by Artie. He dragged his feet with us, refused to answer many questions but did say he said he was an insurance salesman making cold calls…and then the mouthpiece walked through the door."

"You couldn't hold him."

Frank shook his head. "We didn't have enough. He and his major-league lawyer walked out the door, Mr. Burns got in a cab and got on his plane, I assume, and that was the last we ever saw of him."

"Did you follow up on the information you did have?"

"Sure. Guess what. We couldn't find any trace of an insurance man named Arthur Burns from Waukegan or anywhere else. We turned up a few guys with the name but they didn't match."

"What about the lawyer who sprung him?"

"He was an out-of-town guy too, up from the Los Angeles area. A partner in a firm that we later figured had some dubious connections of its own with murky figures. We tried to contact him, but he refused to talk with us about the event. Simply said it was a closed deal: we had picked up an innocent man, and that was that. Wouldn't divulge how he had been connected with or contacted by our suspect. In the end Artie Burns was just dust in the wind."

"One that got away. You were sure you had the right guy."

"We had the sense he was good for it. You know the feeling. Nothing else we pursued ever panned out in any way near as right. We only got surer of it as time went by. We picked up rumors that Lon had run afoul of some organization types back East in New England and that they had taken some steps when they got worried about his possibly turning snitch."

"That's quite a story, Detective."

"Call me Frank. I'm just a citizen here in your territory."

"So what is it about this guy that makes you so sure Artie Burns could have been Barry Fields? You said the eyes?"

Frank nodded. "I was only in the room with him for fifteen minutes at best, probably less. He couldn't have said more than fifty, sixty words to us. But he had that snake gaze I mentioned to you before. Icy cold intelligence. I could believe he was a stone killer. He just felt capable of it."

"But otherwise, you said he looked different from this guy Barry Fields?"

"Very different. He had that thick mustache but otherwise he was clean-shaven. As I recall, his hair was fuller and darker. He had an ordinary dark brown suit, the kind of thing you'd expect an insurance salesman to wear. No glasses."

"Height and weight about right?"

"It's been a while, but yeah, I'd say so. I stood alongside Burns and I stood alongside Fields and it was the same angle, more or less."

"So, assuming this guy Burns was your out-of-town killer and he had arranged the accident that killed Shumer, any luck tracing down the alias, if it had been used before?"

"Zero on that. The guy was experienced. Likely he assumed a new identity every time he went out, altered his appearance in simple ways, obtained documentation then got rid of it all upon his exit. Our one lead was that he likely had been recruited by the Boston mob. We did some research into alleged activities by the guy we were told had it in for Lon Shumer. We talked to law enforcement in that area, even Feds. We found three other suspicious deaths over a five-year period. Nothing that could be pinned on anyone, but there were things that stood out in those cases."

"Such as?"

"They were all apparent accidents. Nobody had been shot, stabbed, strangled, or beaten to death. One was a boating accident, a guy who was said to be an excellent swimmer. One was a guy whose car stalled on a railroad track in front of an oncoming train. One was an electrocution in the home with nobody else around."

"And they all gave cause for suspicion, you say. Interesting."

"All three could be traced back to the Boston mob guy, maybe a little tenuously, but the connection was always there. They happened in different cities but all three times local law enforcement was hesitant to close the door on the deaths."

"So you began to suspect that this Artie Burns guy was behind these accidents. He was, like you said, a professional fixer."

"Nothing anybody could prove. Cops in different places sharing instincts. But I'm not a fan of the concept of coincidence."

"Which leads me to the next question. Assuming Barry Fields is the same guy, he could only be in Easton on an assignment."

Maravich left the remainder of the thought hanging in the air for a long moment.

"And lo and behold," Frank finally said, "you have this remarkable accidental death only the night before."

Maravich crossed his hands over his chest, took a deep breath and sighed heavily. "Lord help us. Sheriff Riculla is not ready to believe Ralph Watkins was anything but an accident."

"Tell me a little bit about it, if you can? What exactly do they think happened?"

"Ralph closes his station every evening around dinner time. Maybe five or six. He was a bit of a hermit, kept to himself mostly, turned up now and then at the diner or the bar or at a store or market, but usually just kept to himself. He lived a ways down the road from the station in an old farmhouse. Anyway, the prevailing wisdom is that he decided to have himself a few nips before going home and possibly got too involved in that undertaking. From the evidence, it looks as if he sat himself down out front of his station too near the pumps and lit himself up a cigar. There was a leak or a spill from the pump and...*boom!* Explosion that could be heard a block away. Big fire. By the time the fire department got to him, he was burned almost beyond recognition."

"So if he had been assaulted in any way, let's say for the sake of argument, knocked unconscious...there would have been no evidence left on his body since it was burned up."

"For the sake of argument, correct. If there were reason to suspect said assault, of course."

"No question it was Ralph, though, right?"

"Dental records confirmed it. One thing Ralph did do was visit the doc and the dentist regularly."

"How are they so sure he was drunk and was smoking? I told you, I had a brief conversation with him earlier that same day and he told me he had sworn off both."

"They actually found remnants of the cigar and pieces of the bottle. It was pretty clear."

Frank covered his eyes with his hand and thought for a moment. Still holding that position, he asked, "Any idea what kind of cigar and what kind of booze?"

Maravich pulled a manila folder out from under his notepad and pulled out some papers, leafing through them. "Nobody's gone to the trouble of identifying the remnants of the cigar. The bottle was amber-colored and square. Black label."

"Ever see a bottle of Rebel Jim bourbon?"

"Probably. Can't quite picture it. Wait a second." Maravich hit Frank's wavelength all at once. His eyes widened.

"It's a square, amber-tinted bottle with a narrow neck about three inches long. Black label. That's what Barry Fields was buying at the gift shop. Along with a couple of cigars."

Maravich picked up a phone and asked the operator for a number.

"Marge, hi, it's Lee over at the Sheriff's. I asked you not to disturb Mr. Fields' room yet…great, nobody's been in there? Nothing's been cleaned or removed? That's real good. I'm going to be over in a little while, okay? Do me another favor, don't empty any of the garbage bins around the lodge until I get a chance to look things over? Thanks."

The deputy hung up and looked at Frank. "I'm hoping to be wrong, but I'm thinking we are not going to find a whiskey bottle or any remains of a cigar in Mr. Fields' room. Or disposed of anywhere around the lodge."

"So you're starting to think I might not be crazy about Ralph Watkins, then," Frank said.

"Why would some gangster type come out here to kill old Ralph?" Maravich asked. "And then why would he get killed himself? This is still crazy. Maybe it all is just a bunch of strange coincidences."

"As I said," Frank replied, "in my experience there is no such thing. Maybe your experience has been different."

The deputy chewed on that for a bit and began to shake his head slowly back and forth. "No sir. It has not. Things generally happen for a reason, once all the facts are in."

"Once all the facts are in," Frank nodded. "What do you really know about Ralph Watkins anyway?"

"Not much. He moved here maybe two, three years ago. Bought that old farmhouse and service station. He was a good mechanic."

"Did he ever tell anyone where he came from, why he moved here? I mean no offense to this lovely town, but this is kind of off the beaten path."

"He said he came here to forget. That, in essence, is what he's told anyone nosing into his affairs. Nobody seems to have gotten many details but he said he lost his family in a terrible tragedy and came here to forget. He's always been a nice enough sort, just kept himself at arm's length from everybody who tried to get close."

"Apparently my ex-wife was one of those people trying to make a reclamation project out of him."

"Muriel was fond of lost puppies and kittens, even the human sort, that is true. But you knew that."

"Oh yeah. That was her all right. And when the kindness wasn't in gear, the curiosity was. I can see her trying to get the goods on Ralph Watkins. But she apparently didn't succeed either, so the guy was a regular clam, it would seem."

"Yes he was."

"Whatever was in his past, he seems to have had reason to keep it bottled up. In a manner of speaking."

"And you say he told you he wasn't drinking anymore?"

"Or smoking."

"I'll do some asking around, but I don't know that anyone has talked about seeing him at the roadhouse tavern of late."

"Father McNulty, over at the church, told me much the same thing. He was sure that Ralph wasn't drinking anymore also. This whole thing bothered him as well."

"I'll make a point to go speak with the Padre tonight after I go back to the Sportsman."

"One other thing, you said there were some other people asking questions about Ralph's death?"

"Oh yeah. They really put a bug up Rick Riculla's ass. They're driving him crazy. They also got a team in a van that sealed off the service station today, just came in and took over. They even sent our deputies away, and they were not nice about it. That's a way to get on his bad side for sure."

"Would they be the man and woman in the dark suits I saw with the Sheriff earlier?"

"The same."

"They look like FBI to me. I don't suppose…"

"Actually," Maravich said, "they're Federal Marshals."

"Marshals? Really?"

"Rick told me he's got no idea why they're here or what they want, but he seems a little tentative about that and I wonder. They seem to agree with him that the death was accidental. But they're asking around, an awful lot of questions. You'll likely see them. They must be staying at the Sportsman too."

"Marshals. I'm thinking what you find Federal Marshals doing."

"Don't see them much around here. They transport prisoners, don't they? And run down fugitives."

"Something else they do, Deputy."

"Uh huh, and that would be?…"

"They run the Federal Witness Protection Program."

FOUR

"I'm just gonna quick clear off the dishes here. Why don't you go sit in the living room? I'll be right in."

"Sure I can't give you a hand with those, Francis?"

"Naw, I'm just gonna pile them up in the kitchen and throw 'em in the dishwasher later. Then I'm gonna visit the jake for a moment and make myself an after-dinner drink. Can I bring you one?"

"No, thanks," Frank said, rising from the table. Half a bottle of wine was more than he usually drank. Francis had also had a couple of stiff shots before dinner. Frank had to give him some slack on that. This had not been a good day for him and he seemed to be carrying its full weight. "Hey, great steaks."

That brought a smile. "Hadn't used the barbecue in a while. Guess I haven't lost my touch."

"Not by my lights." Frank wandered into the living room and aimed himself at a comfortable-looking stuffed chair.

"Be right back. Make yourself at home."

Frank looked around the room and spotted what looked like a school yearbook on a nearby coffee table. He picked it up and sat down in the chair. It was every bit as comfortable as it had looked to be.

The yearbook turned out to be from Lafferty College in Massachusetts from some years back. On a hunch he leafed through the section on seniors and found a picture of one "Frank Lansdowne," a younger and more callow version of his host. It made him smile. He browsed through more of the section at a series of unfamiliar names and faces.

"I see you found my old Lafferty yearbook."

"Yeah, you had it out on the table. Amazing to think how young we all were once, isn't it?"

Francis sat down on the sofa across from Frank and placed a tall glass on the table. It was full of amber liquid and ice cubes. "Uh-huh. I was reminiscing the other day and pulled it out."

Frank closed the book and put it on the table in front of him. "So you went to school on the East Coast. Lafferty's a good school."

Francis nodded. "I was lucky to get in. Even got some financial aid."

"What did you major in?"

"Business. I planned to move to someplace like New York or Boston and become a world beater."

"That plan would seem to have changed."

"Right after school I got an entry-level job in a firm in Connecticut, but then my dad got sick. He ran a hardware and automotive supply business. I decided to come back home and help rescue the two stores. After he passed away, I stayed on. I still run them today."

"And it was after that that you met Muriel here."

"Well, we knew each other in high school, though we were a couple years apart. When she moved back here, she came to work for the stores, doing our bookkeeping...and we got re-acquainted."

Frank nodded with a smile. "And the rest is history."

"Guess so."

"Did she continue to work for you after that?"

"Naw. That was kind of something to tread water for her. She really wanted to teach. She taught middle school for a while, ran the school library."

"She went back to teaching. That's interesting. What was her subject?"

"English, social studies…kinda fits in with her interests and all."

"Definitely. That's what she was doing when we were married, teaching junior high, or middle school, as they call it now. Then the system started to grind her down. In some ways, being in the public school system in a big city is similar to what I do. A lot of banging your head against a wall. But Muriel had a lot more idealism than I do, I guess, and got tired of that constant Quixotic struggle with the bureaucracy. She decided to give it up and go back to school. I guess she picked up accounting along the way."

In fact Muriel had still been in school when they split up. He realized he hadn't even known what courses she took. The memories made him uncomfortable. He found himself gazing around the room. "This was her family's house?"

"Uh-huh. When her folks passed away, she inherited it. It made sense for us to move in here. Much nicer and roomier than my old place."

"It looks as if you two were very happy together. That's a good thing."

"We were, Frank. We really were."

"She deserved to be happy. I'm afraid I wasn't a very good husband on that score."

"For what it's worth, I never—well, let's say almost never—heard complaints from Muriel. What she did say about you was almost entirely good."

"I keep hearing that, but…really?"

"If she spoke about your marriage at all, she mostly would say it hadn't been meant to go on, and she'd leave it at that."

Frank leaned forward and rested his elbows on his thighs. He sat pensive for some time, staring at the carpet, and finally spoke.

"You probably know she came out West to go to school. After she graduated was when she met me. I had just been promoted to Detective. I guess she thought I seemed…dashing or exciting or something."

"She told me about meeting you. Some kind of break-in at her apartment."

"Right. A burglary. I was just taking facts, investigating. A couple of months later we caught the guy. He was a druggie hitting the neighborhood apartments. I went back to fill her in and asked her out for coffee."

"I suspect that wasn't something you did with every single burglary victim."

Frank just raised his eyebrows and smiled a little.

"And the rest is history," Francis said, returning a smile of his own.

"There you go."

"Muriel had this big interest in crime and cops and mysteries and the whole thing. She loved mystery stories and crime fiction."

"Yes she did. I think it came as a disappointment to her just how prosaic the real thing is. How time consuming and frustrating."

"She said she got you into watching mysteries on TV and reading them, because you liked to deconstruct them and tell her exactly how inaccurate they were."

Frank shook his head and sighed loudly. "That was me. You know, I still do that. She got me hooked on those damned things. Just so I can go, 'Ah-*hah!* Got *that* wrong too!' Kind of crazy."

He looked up at Francis. "She must have told you about all the nights I wasn't there. Even when I was home. Too much in my head."

"Yeah. A little bit. But I think she understood, Frank. That was your life. She always said you cared. You cared about the victims. About the job. About doing the right thing. And she always said that was hard for you."

"It's hard for all of us who do what I do. You see all kinds of things…the depths people can sink to. You honestly do want to make a difference. There are always obstacles and roadblocks. As I said, the best it can be is really frustrating. At worst it's straight out dehumanizing. There's that temptation to feel sorry for yourself, to start to think that nobody understands. But what was harder for me to realize, was that wasn't the real issue. The real issue was that whether or not she understood, I couldn't be available for her. I couldn't be there."

He looked down again. "Not even when I *was* there. Physically, I mean. It began to dawn on me that maybe I was incapable of being there for anybody else. In the end, it was clear cut what we had to do."

"Did she ever tell you about me? I mean, after she moved back here and all."

"We didn't communicate much after she returned to Easton. She sent me a couple of letters, we had maybe a couple of phone calls. In what, nine or ten years?"

"We would have been married eight years this August. So yeah, that would be about when she moved back here."

"Funny, one of the few things I remember her telling me was that you liked cigars. That, and that you owned a hardware store."

"Two stores, actually. They're next door to one another along Main Street. Yes, our main drag is actually called Main Street. And there's an Elm Street and a Maple Street too. Like something out of a story, huh?"

"In fact there's a West Elm and an East Elm," Frank said, remembering the address of the Theodore Rollins Funeral Home.

"On either side of Main. Also a West and East Maple. And Oak. And Sycamore. The founding fathers were optimistic." They both laughed a little. "Anyway, the stores are called Lands Hardware and Lands Automotive. My dad figured shortening the name gave it a better recognition factor."

"So when did you stop being Frank and become Francis?"

"When I left college. I figured it gave me more, I don't know, gravitas or something. My mother used to call me Francis. When I went to college, I wanted to be different so I told people I was Frank. I hung out with a bunch of frat boys in school and when that was over, I figured it was time to get more serious. Something like that. I haven't gone by Frank in many years."

"Just as well," said Frank. "It might have been confusing this week, between us both."

"True. Confusing enough as it was."

"So, all those guys you partied with in college, how did they all turn out?"

"Some of them went back to take over their family businesses too. But they weren't hardware stores in the Midwest; they were, like, law firms and ad agencies. There were even a couple of guys from mob families, and heaven knows what they wound up doing."

"A number of those kinds of guys would send their kids to school to get them out of the business, get them into something legitimate."

"Could be. I never kept in touch with anyone from those years. Once I got back here I burned my bridges. In fact I almost never left town again. There was our honeymoon, when Muriel and I went to the Bahamas. That was about it. Aside from that, I've been here in Easton and never felt the need to go anywhere else."

After a short silence, Frank changed the subject.

"I'm just curious. Did Ralph Watkins ever buy automotive parts or stuff like that from you?"

"Oh, sure. All the time."

"Did you guys talk much?"

Francis shrugged. "Probably as much as anybody did with Ralph. He was friendly enough but not much on talking."

"Did he say much about his past, his family, anything?"

"Not really. He once said he came here to forget. Never anything more specific than that. I gathered that something traumatic happened to him. Maybe he lost his family in an accident or something, or maybe there was a really harsh divorce. There was just him, living in that house and running that gas station."

"I would think sooner or later a man living all alone like that would find the need for someone to talk to, you know?"

"Well, Ralph did drink a bit, at least when he first came out here. He hung out at the local watering hole some evenings. On occasion I'd stop by there after a particularly bad day at the store, or like that, and I'd sometimes see him there. Seemed as if he mostly watched whatever sports were on and talked inconsequential stuff with the guys at the bar. If he had a confidant or a close friend, I sure never knew about it."

"Or a girlfriend or something, you know?"

Francis took another gulp from his drink and raised his eyebrows. "I know. You'd think."

"It seems that Muriel thought along similar lines, huh? She wanted to fix him up with someone?"

"Yeah. She tried to make a reclamation case out of old Ralph. She talked about inviting him to groups she was involved with, and so forth. He wasn't having any part of it."

"Did she ever try to introduce him to anyone specific? I could see Muriel doing that, you know?"

Francis laughed. "Yeah, yeah. For sure. No, she talked about it, tried bouncing various ideas off of me. 'What about so-and-so, think they'd get along?' I never encouraged her. My feeling was always that Ralph wanted to be alone, needed to work out whatever it was he needed to work out, and we should respect that. She never acted on any of that, just talked it over with me and her other friends."

"Sounds like she learned a bit about Ralph's background after all. Like that TV character we were talking about, the detective's wife."

"Ha! Yeah. I do think she tried different ploys to get him to drop some little bits of information to her, but I doubt she ever succeeded. Ralph was elusive. Downright slippery when he wanted to be. And, when you come down to it, people in this town respect privacy. I don't know if you've ever lived in a really small rural town like Easton?"

"Nope. I grew up in the city. Urban all my life."

"There's this strange and charming dichotomy. On the one hand, we're a small village and everybody knows everybody else and everybody has this sense of protectiveness and togetherness. We're like a family. Or a tribe. It's hard to do anything without everyone else knowing about it right away. But then on the other hand, there's a sense of respecting limits. There's a line past which you don't ever go. Someone else's business is theirs and theirs alone. That's a sort of family thing as well. You don't find either one observed quite so strictly in a large city."

Frank nodded. "So a guy like Ralph couldn't quite hide, but he could be sort of anonymous in plain sight."

"Something like that, yeah."

Francis had unearthed a box of photos earlier and they looked through them, passing them back and forth. Francis told stories and gave background and seemed to lighten his own mood considerably. It was surprisingly not very awkward for Frank at all. The evening turned out to be a comfortable one. Finally Frank looked at his watch and began to make his good-byes, thanking Francis for dinner and the company.

"Frank, something I need to tell you," Francis said as they rose.

"What's that?"

"Clearly there's something that's been on your mind about you and Muriel. I don't know exactly what it might be, but believe me you should put it to rest. You did okay by her, Frank. You couldn't give her what you didn't have to give. You did the best you could. Muriel understood that." He looked Frank straight in the eye and extended his hand.

"Thanks, Francis." They shook hands and he turned to leave.

* * * *

When Frank finally pulled into the parking lot of the Sportsman, he saw several people congregating around a dark sedan and a van parked nearby. The man and woman he had seen earlier at the Sheriff's station were among them, now in dark windbreakers rather than suits. Large yellow letters on the back proclaimed U. S. MARSHAL in bold. They all looked as if it had been a long day.

The woman spotted Frank as he got out of his car, made a comment to her partner, and they approached him. They were both dark-haired and serious.

The woman spoke when they were a few feet away. "Excuse me, you're Detective Vandegraf, I believe?"

"Around here, I'm just plain Frank Vandegraf, but yes."

She produced a folding case with ID and a badge. "I'm Deputy United States Marshal Candace Maldonado. This is Deputy United States Marshal Franco Bartolli. Could we have a moment of your time?"

Frank sighed. It had been a long day for him as well, and all he really wanted was some sleep. "Sure."

"We understand you've been asking about last night's incident involving the nearby service station fire and death of the owner."

"I've talked about it with a couple of people, yes."

"May I ask your interest in the incident?" Maldonado, Frank noted, appeared quite at home with the scowl that seemed set on her face. Bartolli maintained a similar grimace and said nothing.

"Driving in yesterday, I stopped at the station and had a very brief conversation with the owner, Ralph Watkins. In the course of that conversation he happened to mention that he had stopped drinking and smoking. Subsequently, I heard that his death was attributed to an accident caused by his drinking heavily and carelessly lighting a cigar near his gas pumps. It just struck me as odd, and I happened to mention that to some people I encountered here in Easton."

"You went to the Sheriff's Department and discussed it with a deputy."

"I did. As you know, I'm a police detective. I did what I would have wanted someone in my own jurisdiction to do if they thought they had information that might be of interest in the investigation."

"Have you ever had any other communication with Ralph Watkins at any time?"

"Nope. We exchanged a few sentences when I gassed up. That was it."

Maldonado eyed him carefully. "And who else have you shared this observation with?"

"Just one or two people who knew him." He left it at that.

Bartolli finally piped up. "We understand you've also been talking about another individual that you encountered here, who was involved in a separate incident today?"

"You mean Barry Fields. He was a guest here at the lodge and we also exchanged a few words. That was it. I mentioned that as well to the Deputy Sheriff when I was at the station."

"You seem to be showing a lot of interest in the goings-on around here."

Frank tried to mask his growing impatience. "As I said, I simply came forward to offer whatever small information I might have. That's it."

Maldonado took over once again. "Detective, can you tell us exactly why you're here?"

Frank returned Maldonado's scowl along with a steady stare for a very long moment before replying. "I came here to bury my ex-wife. But I think you knew that already, didn't you?"

Maldonado waited a beat or two before her own answer. "My condolences for your loss, sir. May we assume you'll be leaving soon?"

"I actually would have been gone by now, but I moved my flight. I'm departing Sunday."

"It seems surprising you're staying around that long."

"It was the soonest they could give me. Believe me, I've got no interest in hanging around here any longer than I need to. I seem to be getting diminishing returns on my stay." He maintained his own steadfast glare back at the Marshals.

"All right. Your willingness to come forward and contribute what you know is greatly appreciated, Detective. There happens to be an ongoing investigation and we're sure you can appreciate the need for it to be free of any outside interference."

"Interference has never been my intention," Frank said. It came out more abrupt than he had planned.

"I'm sure you understand that we're conducting an ongoing *con-*

fidential investigation. There is also quite a bit of which you are, necessarily, *not* aware, and we need to keep it that way."

"Of course, Deputy." He evenly moved his gaze from Maldonado to Bartolli and back again.

He considered asking a few more questions, bringing up the subject of witness protection, but definitely thought better of it. He momentarily considered expounding upon his suspicions about Barry Fields, but quickly dismissed that thought as well. He simply let the silence hang awkwardly.

They all exchanged a few more meaningful looks before Maldonado nodded and said tersely, "Thank you, sir. I think we understand each other then. Have a good night."

Neither made an effort to shake Frank's hand. They walked away to join the rest of the Marshals and Frank turned toward his own room.

Suddenly, out of nowhere, something struck him. Funny how that worked.

You toss something around in your mind, worry it to death, can't grasp some elusive fact or detail. Then you leave it alone. Your brain keeps working on it in the background. Frank referred to it as "putting it on the back burner," where it would keep roiling until suddenly something fell into place.

He remembered why Ralph Watkins had seemed familiar to him.

He glanced back at Maldonado and Bartolli and their companions as they walked to their own rooms.

He was sure he had it.

FIVE

As tired as he was, his racing brain would not allow him to rest. Frank finally got to sleep but it was fitful. He set an alarm to be up reasonably early Saturday morning. There were things he wanted to do.

After breakfast he found Marge behind the reception counter. "Don't you ever take a day off?"

She smiled. "Good morning, Mr. Vandegraf. Oh, I'm just watching out for things until Julius comes in for his weekend shift. When you run the business, things never stop."

"That's true."

"So what can I do for you this morning?"

"I was wondering if there's a computer available somewhere, where I can go on the internet."

"You know you've got free wi-fi in your room, right?"

"Unfortunately that won't help me since I don't have a laptop with me." In fact, Frank didn't even own one, but he figured it wasn't worth going into. "Maybe there's a library nearby, or you've got one here?"

"Sure, we have a business center with two internet ready computers." She reached under the counter and brought out a key attached to a small plastic plate. "Honestly, calling it a 'business center' is kind of ambitious. There's a small conference table, a couple of terminals, that type of thing. It's really not very big, but just your luck, it's all yours today."

"Thank you. I might need it a while."

"Shouldn't be a problem. It's the room right down the hall on your right." She scrawled some numbers on a slip of paper and passed it over to him. "Here's your username and password."

"Great. And I figure I can find a small notebook in the gift shop, right?"

* * * *

"Well, fancy meeting you here."

Frank turned around from the monitor and closed the notebook in which he had been feverishly jotting. "Well, Deputy. Looking for me by any chance?"

Maravich pulled up a chair and sat down. "Marge told me you'd be back here. I came over to investigate about our friend Mr. Fields some more, but I also wanted to have another chat with you. You know, fill you in on developments, see if you've got any other input that might be of help."

"I'm assuming this is not at the behest of Sheriff Riculla."

Maravich raised his eyebrows. "My personal behest solely, that's correct."

"After last night, I have the distinct idea that my 'input' isn't all that welcome around here."

"Ahh. I gather you met up with the Marshals then? They do seem to be a piece of work, don't they? They've been really giving Rick Riculla a hard time, too. Even got somebody from back in D.C. to call him, and more than once. He just wants to see them gone and this whole thing over and done." Maravich glanced at the computer screen. "You don't strike me as a man with a lot of social media going on."

"Nope. My twentieth birthday is well past, I fear."

"So I'm thinking you're still doing some research into things we talked about?"

"Back home I have a bit of a reputation among my colleagues as a caveman. Not very accomplished in the digital world. I've got an old flip phone and I don't have a laptop. But I figured I'd navigate my way around a few things this morning just to kill some time since I'm a captive audience here until my flight tomorrow. I can do that, find my way around cyberspace with a little blundering and a little luck."

"And how's that working out?" The deputy smiled.

"I have a colleague back in my squad, Jill Garvey, who's technically very savvy. She's always kidding me about being a Luddite. She'd be proud of me today. I am actually finding things. Sometimes I surprise myself."

"What kind of things?"

"Just answering a couple questions that were bugging me. What can I tell you? I'm just a cop. I'll be gone and out of your hair pretty soon, and whatever I give you is yours to do with as you please."

Maravich shook his head and looked weary. "I don't know that anything is going to be of much use, to be honest with you. I'm finding myself up against what I guess you'd call politics and such. I might be grasping at straws when all is said and done. But I'm happy to take whatever you've got, in any case."

"I've got a few things we can talk about. But first, Deputy, I have a question for you."

"Shoot."

"Is there any possibility that Muriel Lansdowne's death was not an accident?"

Maravich crossed his arms, shook his head and laughed quietly. "Frank, you really are trying to stir up trouble around here, aren't you?"

"It's just I've never been a big fan of coincidence. I think we talked about that before. In the past few days, you've probably had more deaths than you've seen in quite a while, isn't that true? I mean, *curious* deaths."

Maravich stared at Frank with a small smile on the corners of his mouth. It seemed he was trying to decide whether to take him seriously or not.

"Frank Vandegraf comes to town and all hell breaks loose."

"Really. Has the Department given it any consideration at all?"

"That Muriel's death was a homicide, you mean? That's a stretch. A big stretch." He shook his head again and looked at the ground in thought. "No. She fell off a ladder. There's nothing that would indicate anything else."

"It's just a little odd. Francis said he was surprised she would go up on that ladder by herself. What if someone else was there with her?"

"The only person that comes to mind would be Francis himself. Are you suggesting he killed his wife?"

"I don't know what I'm suggesting. There's just something off there."

"Frank, here we are back at coincidences again, and I'm still no fan of them, but sometimes things just happen. I just don't see it." Maravich directed his gaze back at Frank. "In fact that's one of the things I came here to tell you about. Damnedest thing."

"Should we maybe go get a cup of coffee or something and talk? Then we can come back here and maybe I can show you some things."

"Sounds good to me. The restaurant here has much better coffee than the station, that's a fact."

* * * *

Maravich thanked the waitress for his mug of steaming coffee and took an appreciative sip. "So here's the strange thing I was starting to tell you about. I told you we found footprints and what looked like a knee print on the embankment of that first overpass."

"I remember."

"We also found shells. Not just one or two. Nine altogether."

"Twenty-twos?"

"Yes. And what looks like the last remains of a marijuana joint, what the kids call a roach. And an empty potato chip bag and an empty soda can."

"Hardly sounds like a professional shooter to me."

"It certainly does not. But there's more."

Frank took a sip of his own coffee and leaned forward, fascinated by this bizarre new development.

"I think I mentioned that we found two other slugs on the other side of the roadway. One was in a tree, one in another embankment. Our guys found another one lodged in the concrete of the overpass."

"Okay."

"And then there's this. We got a call yesterday from a lady named Charice Barnes. She lives a couple miles from here and she's a registered nurse, what you call a traveling nurse. Right now she's working at Mercy General Hospital, which is about forty miles down the road. That same road. She has to get up very early for her shift and drives that way."

"So you're saying she was on the road around the same time as Barry Fields yesterday morning."

"It seems so, yes. Coroner hasn't established the exact time of death yet but it seems safe that it was around four A.M. Charice was coming through there somewhere around that time."

"Okay."

"She told us she heard a loud noise against the side of her car. She was alone in the dark on a deserted stretch of road, so she was scared to stop and investigate. I don't blame her. Her car seemed to be driving okay so she kept going all the way to the hospital. Once she felt safe in the lighted parking lot, she checked out her car. There was a bullet hole in her right rear fender."

"A bullet hole."

"That's right. She called us after her shift and we had her bring the car over for us to take a look at. The bullet was there, in the trunk of her car."

"And it was a twenty-two, I'm guessing."

Maravich nodded.

"We've got footprints from a hunting boot, a knee print that looks to be from jeans, and a soda can we can pull prints off. There's a local family with two teenage kids who are a little bit off, shall we say. We've had trouble with them a few times."

"You're thinking your hit man got killed by a kid taking pot shots off the embankment in the middle of the night?"

"By the way, we can't be sure that he was a hit man yet. But yes… there were complaints about one of the boys doing something similar a month or two ago."

Frank rubbed the back of his neck. "So you're saying at this point it's looking like everything's a grand coincidence of weird events."

"I'm saying only that it's the most consistent with the evidence. We follow the evidence, am I right?"

"I can't argue that. Of course you do. It's just…"

"I know. It's strange."

"I assume you've been talking to the boys in question."

"A couple deputies went by their home last night and brought them in. Lem and Lyle. A little history of trouble with both boys, nothing all that serious. The whole family's a little off. Their father was a vet, came back from overseas with post-traumatic stress syndrome. But maybe I'm telling tales out of school now."

"One or both of them own twenty-twos, I'm guessing?"

Maravich nodded. "Several weapons in that family, including a couple twenty-twos. We have them in custody."

Frank shook his head. "A kid sitting near a bridge late at night, shooting at random passing cars and trucks. Could that really be all of it?"

"As soon as we've matched up the slugs and shells to one of the guns, I suspect, yes."

Frank chewed on that for a while. "It still doesn't explain what that Barry Fields guy was doing here. Or why he checked out and was leaving in the dead of the night."

"I have to agree. One possibility is he really was who he said he was, a guy representing that company Irrawaddy, and he was on his way to do some more location scouting. But…"

"But?" Frank prompted.

Maravich looked abashed. "We've tried to find out more about him, to try to contact next of kin and so forth. So far it's a dead end."

"Is the company real?"

"There's a real website, at any rate, but it's just got a place-holder image at the moment, just says 'Coming soon, watch this site!' and some other things to that effect."

"And let me venture a guess: his card didn't have a telephone number?"

"He had written his cell number on a few of the cards. That was it."

"Have you checked out his phone? You said it was a burner of some sort."

"Yep. The number matched. Bought it with prepaid minutes at the airport. The kind you can add more minutes to if you want, with a credit card."

"That's kind of weird for a sales rep or whatever, wouldn't you say?"

"I'd say so. But some of these internet startups are pretty unorthodox. Slippery folks. I'm sure you've encountered the people I mean, right?"

"Yes," Frank sighed. "Yes, I have."

"Running on hope and promises. Need to come across impressive. They've got no money, but want to make it look as if they do, so they run on the cheap but try to make it all look slick and corporate. It's all hat and no cattle, like some of my relatives down in Texas like to say."

"I think you're giving this guy a huge benefit of the doubt, Deputy."

"I'm just trying to stay objective, Frank. But my doubt grows by the minute as we're unable to find any trace of somebody named Barry Fields."

"And suppose he wasn't who he said he was? Then what are the alternatives?"

"Your suggestion certainly has to stay in play."

"That he came here to eliminate Ralph Watkins."

"There are a lot of people not liking that idea, let me tell you. But yes, I have to keep it in mind."

Frank downed the remainder of his coffee and picked up the check lying on the table. "Come on back to the computer with me. I've got some things to show you that you might find interesting."

* * * *

The newspaper was about three and a half years old, and the front page filled the screen. The headline screamed in huge dark type across the top of the page.

TESTIMONY NAILS MOB BOSS

Maravich scanned the article rapidly. "Pat Fine. I remember reading about him. One of the big shots in the New England organization."

Frank scrolled down on the page to a photo at the bottom. Its caption read TESTIMONY OF FINE UNDERLING LARRY WARNECKE PAINTS DAMNING EVIDENCE THAT COULD SEAL HIS FATE.

"Take a good look at that photo. Look familiar?"

"It's not a great reproduction. Hard to tell."

"Right. So then let's go here…"

Frank clicked the mouse a few times and toggled over to another web page. This one was a popular online encyclopedia. The entry read RAYMOND LAWRENCE "LARRY" WARNECKE at the top. The introduction described Warnecke as "a former associate of the Fine crime family. He is known as the man who helped bring down Pat Fine, the family's boss, by agreeing to become a Federal witness." The article continued at some length.

"He was a well-connected guy," Frank said. "Pretty high up in the scheme of things, responsible for collections, the kind of guy who might have possession of incriminating records of various sorts. Something happened to his wife and child. They were in a car that drove off a bridge and they were killed. Warnecke apparently concluded someone in the organization was responsible, possibly Fine himself. It almost seems like it became a personal vendetta between those two. He turned state's evidence with a vengeance."

The deputy nodded, focusing in on the monitor.

"Notice there's no further information on his whereabouts or anything after the date of the trial. And look at the photo at the top."

Maravich's eyes moved back and forth, up and down. His expression grew grave.

"You're thinking this Warnecke became Ralph Watkins?"

"What do you think?"

"I see a resemblance."

"There's also this: relocated witnesses are encouraged to choose a new name that has some memory connection to their old one so they're more comfortable with it—perhaps keep the same first name or initials. You'll note this guy's real name was RAYMOND Warnecke. RW."

"There's no information on this guy after a certain date, and then not long after that, Ralph shows up here in Easton. Okay. That would explain the Marshals."

"You're being a little coy with me, aren't you? I have a feeling you already know Ralph Watkins had an assumed identity."

After a moment of silent consideration, the deputy returned Frank's stare and nodded.

"This is still confidential. Rick Riculla told me last night that Ralph was in Witness Protection. That's all he said, though I could tell he was not happy about that, and I shouldn't even be telling you this at all just yet. It'll probably all come out sooner or later."

Maravich needed an ally, Frank figured. It ran against his grain to be telling what he called stories out of school, but this was his only avenue. And clearly he had decided that Frank could be trusted.

"I had a feeling," Frank said. "You mentioned searching for Fields' next of kin but haven't yet said a word about doing that for Ralph, and I'd think that would mean more to you. I've been doing some reading this morning on the Federal Witness Security program and there's plenty that's very interesting. Their policy is to inform local law enforcement when a relocated protected witness has been placed in their jurisdiction.

"So Sheriff Riculla had to have known about this," he continued. "...though he might not have seen any reason to make that knowledge readily known in the Department and most likely didn't like the whole arrangement in the least. At this time the Marshals won't want to divulge any more than they have to, but in any case they would have to tell the Sheriff *something* about what's up. And now I'd think the Sheriff would need to bring at least a few of his people up to speed, and you seem a likely one. It wouldn't surprise me if they kept Ralph's real identity under wraps for a while longer. But I'm betting when they do let it out, it's going to be Larry Warnecke."

A slight smile pulled at the corners of Maravich's mouth. "Assuming all that is true? It still doesn't mean that Fields was here to kill him."

"Playing devil's advocate, are you?"

"Someone's got to."

"Okay. Fair enough. I'll toss ideas out, you shoot them down."

"Whenever you're ready."

"There were things that would be consistent with Fields coming from the northeast U.S."

"You mean like the expression he used for showing an ID. That's thin, don't you think?"

"Taken by itself, maybe. There's his resemblance to a guy I questioned about a suspected murder related to the Boston mob."

"Again, mighty theoretical. Nothing that would hold up in a courtroom."

"And the remarkable series of 'accidental' deaths of other individuals who fell afoul of the same mob guy who would have hired him."

"Also kind of thin."

"...who happened to be an associate of this Pat Fine guy."

"Nothing here to disprove Fields was what he said he was, though."

"For Pete's sake, Lee! The guy went out of his way to change his appearance before he left! He shaved his beard, changed his hair color, ditched his glasses!"

Maravich's smile grew a bit deeper. "You're telling me he shaved and that his glasses were for looks. Maybe he was just vain or a little obsessive about his appearance. Maybe he was a flim-flam artist with that internet company."

"He bought whiskey and cigars, consistent with what was found at the scene of Ralph's death, and there was no sign of them around his room, am I right?"

"You're looking at this like a crime scene investigator. I'm looking at it like a prosecutor. 'Consistent' is one thing. 'Conclusive' is another. Any prosecutor around here would laugh me out of his office with that kind of conjecture. Where's the solid evidence?"

"It's the whole picture. All the circumstances around Watkins' death. We've gone over that. He wasn't smoking or drinking anymore, and here he supposedly died by getting drunk and playing with cigars. It wasn't characteristic of him, was it?"

"But you can find people around here who remember that it was. Perhaps not recently, but who's to say his good intentions all went up in smoke?"

"No pun intended, I assume," Frank remarked. Maravich chuckled. "And yet Father McNulty claimed pretty stridently that he felt Ralph's resolution to abstinence was firm. Did you talk to him last night?"

"As a matter of fact, I did. I got quite a different story from him."

That stopped Frank in his tracks, just when he was rolling. "Huh? What do you mean?"

"He said he couldn't be sure just what state of mind Ralph might have been in. He couldn't authoritatively state if Ralph was on the wagon or drinking. That was about all he'd say."

"You've gotta be kidding!"

The deputy shrugged.

"So at this point all I've got on that is your statement that you heard him claim, in a casual exchange, that he wasn't drinking or smoking any more. Again, that's not much to hang anything on. There's no evidence of any kind of wrongful death. Nothing that that prosecutor I mentioned would accept and not laugh me out of the office."

"The priest clammed up! Why would he do that? He was pretty insistent when I spoke with him."

"Let me ask you something else, Frank. How did you come up with this Warnecke guy to begin with? Where's the connection?"

"I might have mentioned to you earlier, when I stopped at Ralph Watkins' gas station, I had this feeling he looked familiar in some odd way. I couldn't put my finger on it. After I had the same experience with Barry Fields, I just figured I was experiencing away-from-home syndrome, where you want to see something or someone familiar, so your mind starts playing tricks on you, you know?"

"Uh huh. But?…"

"The connection came to me quicker about Fields, and I still think I nailed his identity correctly. Watkins was more subtle. But it was something about his voice, his mannerisms, that rang a bell."

"So you had spoken with this other guy, Warnecke, at some point?"

"No. I watched videos of his testimony."

"Videos." Maravich raised his eyebrows. "You mean like on the news?"

"No. We were looking into the possible connections in the Shumer case I told you about, and a couple of others, with the New England mob. Like I told you before, we don't like wise guys trying to move in from out of town."

"So you were doing research on possible figures involved in the move?"

"Exactly. We consulted with an agent in the FBI's Organized Crime program, a pretty sharp guy named Gary Hedges."

"Hedges, you say?"

"Right. As in 'trimming.' "

"Or 'bets,' maybe."

"Whatever. He provided us with all kinds of background, including on Warnecke and other characters on that scene. We had Federal law enforcement footage on the testimony, among lots of other resources. There was just something about the way this Warnecke guy spoke. He was nervous, self-conscious. He kind of twitched his head in odd ways, like an insect."

Maravich seemed to think of something. He nodded briefly.

"Is that ringing any of those bells with you, Deputy? Sound like Ralph Watkins?"

"Nothing concrete. Just a couple of times I recall he got a little upset about something or other, and he'd get kind of...you used the word twitchy?"

Frank nodded. "You know the feeling you get sometimes about something or somebody. In the police academy they taught me to trust those weird hunches."

Maravich nodded. "Me too."

"Where'd you get your training, if you don't mind my asking?"

"My family's from east Texas and Louisiana. I originally applied to be a Texas state trooper. I trained with them before moving up here."

"Wow. Big change."

"Yeah, well, you meet the right person, things happen. Long story. My wife's family is from the next county over, so she had reasons to come back."

"Sounds to me like the Sheriff was lucky to get you."

Maravich shrugged. "Worked out all around."

"Anyway, that's why I'm pretty sure I zoomed in on Ralph Watkins. I think he's really Larry Warnecke. And I think you can see that and in general you agree with me."

Maravich folded his arms, pursed his lips and shook his head. "You might well be right but it's a big leap at this point. You put out a lot of stuff for me here, but it's all conjecture. I'm up against a brick wall. I need something more concrete, Frank."

"Bricks and concrete. Hard stuff indeed. I'll give you everything I've found. We both understand that's the best I can do. The rest is up to your Department. After this weekend I'll be far away."

And somehow, he thought but did not say, that was all for the better. He suddenly had the overwhelming urge to be far, far away from Easton.

"Well," Maravich said, rising from his seat, "hopefully this will be productive. Thanks for your input, Frank. I need to be getting back out there again."

"One last question. Yesterday you referred to a case you never closed that hit close to home."

The deputy nodded.

"If I'm asking anything too personal, feel free to say so, but I was just curious about it."

Maravich took a deep breath before replying. "Carla Rae Jordan."

Frank gave him time.

"We found her behind a road house late one Saturday night. She had been strangled and stuck in a garbage hopper. She was twenty-three."

"Yeah, that sounds like a tough one to deal with. Did you know her? Personally, I mean."

"Her family. My wife knew them. Not well, but she knew them. Carla Rae was the only child."

"Nothing panned out? The leads, I mean?"

"Nope. We had a timeline right up to a couple hours before she died, we interviewed all her friends and associates, covered everything. We finally concluded it was someone from out of town just passing through. We checked for similar crimes in surrounding areas, suspicious individuals, all sorts of things. Nothing." Maravich stared at Frank for a long time. "In the end, the door started to close. It grew colder and colder."

Frank nodded. "I know how that works. Most cases have the best chance of being solved in the first forty-eight hours. You've got a window that lasts a short time and it gets smaller and smaller."

"Yeah. It's not the only case I ever worked on that didn't get resolved. It's just the one that still, to this day, rankles my gut the worst." He shrugged slightly. "Anyway, from that day forth, I've hated like hell to leave any case unclosed. Guess it's the cop in me."

"Guess it's the cop in you for sure."

SIX

At the rectory of St. Dismas' Church, Frank was directed to a quiet garden in a courtyard, where he found Father Kieran McNulty sitting and reading from a small book, likely saying his daily office. He looked up as Frank approached, closed his breviary and smiled.

"Well, fancy meeting you here."

"That's the second time I've heard that this morning, Padre."

"Please, Kieran will do…unless you are here for spiritual guidance of some nature." He gestured for Frank to join him on the oak bench.

"Can't say as that is my reason, Kieran. I'm not really a churchgoing man to begin with."

"Were you ever? Perhaps you were raised a Catholic?"

"My parents were Dutch Reformed, actually. And not great ones at that."

McNulty smiled mischievously. "Then you're not all that far from a bloody Orangeman. You seem a good sort nonetheless."

"And you seem all right yourself for what certain relatives of mine would have called a Papist. Not a hint of rum or Romanism, much less rebellion."

"Well, certainly not the rum anymore, at any rate. I've been known to have a rebellious streak. So what brings you here, Frank?"

"I hope I wasn't disturbing your daily office. I can come back."

"It can keep. The hour's reasonably young."

"I happened to have a conversation with Deputy Sheriff Maravich this morning. He tells me you recanted on your misgivings about the death of Ralph Watkins."

"Recanted. Well. You're going to throw the Inquisition at me next, are you? As it happens, I did *reconsider* some of the comments I shared with you yesterday. I saw no reason to make a mountain out of what was not even a molehill."

"There is a good possibility that Ralph Watkins was living here under an assumed name, that he was a relocated Federal witness, and that all this is going to come out soon."

McNulty nodded, considering this. "None of that would change anything."

"There's a possibility his death was not an accident. And that it's going to be swept under the rug by the Federal authorities."

"And you're saying that my word could change all that?"

"I don't know, Fath...Kieran. It might make a difference. Don't you want to see a crime recognized and justice met?"

"Tell me, Frank, just for the sake of argument: if Ralph's death were to be determined to be a murder, just who do you think might have been responsible?"

"You know about the guy who showed up the day before, don't you?"

"Oh yes. The poor man met with an unfortunate ending himself, did he not? Shot to death on a lonely road, or so I hear. May his soul rest in peace. And again for that same sake of argument, if he was indeed responsible for someone else's death, wouldn't you say he met a form of justice himself? One that might almost be deemed by some, although not myself, to be divine retribution? At very least, that he met a fate that could not be, shall we say, improved upon by a body of law?"

They sat in silence, looking at each other. There was only the rustling of leaves and the chatter of a squirrel in a nearby tree.

"Kieran, we spoke yesterday about the sanctity of the confessional."

"Briefly, yes, we did."

"I find it interesting that Francis Lansdowne wanted to speak with you in the worst way, and now you've changed your mind about all this."

The priest simply stared at Frank, his expression blank.

"I don't have a particularly deep understanding of how the seal of the confessional works. For the sake of argument, as you say...if someone were to confess to you that they had committed a crime, wouldn't you have to divulge that?"

"Solely for the sake of argument." McNulty nodded. "Such a confession would still be a sacred bond. A priest would be strictly bound to say nothing. A priest would strongly urge the penitent to step forward themselves and confess the crime, and to perform whatever restitution was possible to the victims."

"That would be a very difficult position for a moral man of the cloth."

"It comes with the job, lad. I'm sure you're familiar with the responsibilities of lawyers and psychiatrists and such. They deal with similar wrenching situations and do so ethically most every day. One such as myself must answer to a much higher authority in such matters."

"I seem to recall you told me earlier that Ralph Watkins was not a parishioner here at St. Dismas?"

"Heavens no. He was like you, a thoroughly unchurched man, and likely also like yourself, a skeptical sort. That in no way suggests either of you to be anything but ethical and moral, mind you."

Frank laughed. "Of course not."

"I can only tell you this. Ralph and I shared a different bond. I was a counselor of a different sort to him and we shared a different sort of confidentiality."

"You mean you were his twelve-step sponsor."

McNulty considered his answer. "There's no harm, now that he's passed, in shattering that anonymity at least. But whatever was said between us while he lived remains private."

"A different sort of confidentiality," Frank repeated. "He was in the process of making some kind of amends."

"You seem to know a bit about such things."

"I've encountered the program many times. Not personally. My job. Friends. You can't avoid it nowadays, can you?"

"These are all interesting conjectures on your part. It's my policy to neither encourage nor discourage such speculations in any way. I'm sure you understand."

"Father McNulty, remind me never to play poker with you."

They spoke a bit longer before Frank rose from the bench to make his farewells. McNulty said, "Might I ask you a question?"

"Sure."

"Is there a reason you've taken such an interest in the admittedly unusual events of this past week, here in a place a thousand miles from your own home?"

"Good question. I guess I'm just a cop, Kieran. When things don't add up, I just naturally start asking questions."

McNulty nodded. "Would you mind if I asked what theory you have about all these things? I'll offer no editorial comment, but simply listen."

"Why not? Muriel's death strikes me as odd. I have no hard facts on which to base my feeling, but I can't help but wonder if someone else was with her when she took that fall off the ladder."

"Go on."

"It makes no sense. Who might have had a reason to do it? I'm convinced Francis loved her. Everybody in town seems to have loved her. There's nothing concrete to go on."

"Please continue."

"As we talked about yesterday, it struck me as odd that Ralph Watkins had gone out of his way to tell me he neither drank nor smoked, and yet he is said to have gotten drunk and accidentally blown up his service station, and himself, by lighting a cigar. The man that I later encountered in the motel, Barry Fields, reminded me of an individual I personally interviewed on the occasion of another suspicious death a few years ago. And I find that Ralph himself bore a nagging resemblance to a former mobster who turned evidence and subsequently disappeared. His death brought Federal Marshals, a branch that administers Federal Witness Protection, to Easton. All the roads conceivably lead back one way or another to East Coast crime syndicates. It's all curious to me."

McNulty waited and Frank continued.

"I'm thinking that this Barry Fields guy was what you might call a hit man, and that he was dispatched to kill Ralph Watkins, which means that his clients had somehow discovered Ralph's true identity in recent days. How and why this happened now, I've got no ideas. I can't see how it would be connected to Muriel's death but if it were my case to investigate, I also couldn't dismiss the idea entirely."

"And I assume you've told all this to Deputy Maravich."

"Oh yeah. In great detail."

"And what does he say about this?"

"In a nutshell, that it's all conjecture, nothing solid to back up any of it."

"He strikes me as a good man and a good police officer."

"I would say so, yes. A very good one."

"Then I'd say you've suitably discharged your duty, however you might see it."

"Agreed. I'm going home tomorrow, and whatever comes out of this is out of my hands." Frank offered a hand to McNulty, who rose to take it. "I only came here to bury my ex-wife and perhaps bury some ghosts along with her."

"I would hope you have accomplished that as best you could."

"I believe I have. It bothers me that there's a possibility the truth may never come out about her death. But in general I've done all I can do."

"The serenity to accept the things we cannot change, the courage to change what we can, and the wisdom to know the difference," McNulty mused.

"You seem a very accepting man, Kieran, and a thoughtful one. I'd say those are good qualities in a priest."

"I'd say they would be good qualities in any walk of life."

"By the way, it's interesting your parish is named after a thief."

"I'm impressed you knew that, Frank. Dismas was more than a thief. He was a penitent thief, forgiven by Christ himself from the cross. He stands as a lesson to us all that whatever we do, we are capable of being forgiven, if we repent."

There seemed to Frank to be a deeper and more immediate meaning intended in the priest's statement.

They shook hands and nodded at one another.

"God speed on your return trip, Frank. I'll remember you in my prayers today."

"I could probably use them, whether or not I believe in them."

"It's never a question of whether you believe in the divine, lad. The crux of the matter is that it believes in you."

* * * *

Frank decided to drive around a bit. Back on the job, that was often how he allowed his mind to work away at cases. He headed out along the highway where Barry Fields had met his death, figuring he'd be able to recognize the scene when he reached it. He needn't have worried. It was an open stretch of road with mostly farms and a few houses, with few overpasses that were spread apart.

About ten miles out of Easton, he saw two overpasses coming up and as he neared them he saw yellow police tape strung around the first. He slowed as he drove by. There was nobody to be seen, and no other traffic. He pulled over to the side of the road about halfway between the two bridge abutments and stopped his car.

He sat thinking for a few minutes. Only two cars passed before he finally got out of the car and walked back towards the first overpass.

When he was near, he stopped and turned to look at the surroundings. The overpasses were less than a hundred feet apart and apparently carried the two lanes of a divided highway. An occasional car or truck would pass by overhead but generally it was quiet.

Frank could hear the crunch of his footsteps as he resumed walking toward the abutment. When he reached the yellow tape that had been strung around the embankment, he stopped.

Someone could easily drive up from the overhead road, park, and climb down into a position where they could set up a sniper's nest of sorts. He crossed the street, where the opposite abutment had also been cordoned off with yellow tape, and peered over the barrier at the concrete pillars of the bridge. The bridges were relatively new and there wasn't an enormous amount of wear, so he thought it was pretty clear where the bullet hole might be that Maravich had mentioned.

He walked back in the direction of his car then climbed up the bank until he was in the median between the two lanes of the overhead highway. He could see that not far past the bridges in either direction, the lanes converged more closely. He saw more yellow tape sealing off the bridge area here as well.

He stood, hands on hips, for some time, looking at the bridges and thinking.

This didn't strike him as a particularly opportune locale for a professional shooter. Taken along with what Maravich had told him, it certainly seemed that the deputy was right. This was no assassination.

A murder that looked like an accidental death. And now an accidental death that looked like a murder. Could it be?

Frank caught himself in the habitual gesture he always seemed to adopt when he felt puzzled. He was rubbing the back of his neck again. This place was totally crazy.

He headed back into Easton and took the road past the Sportsman's Lodge toward Ralph Watkins' service station. He decided it would not be a good idea to stop or even slow down there, lest he run afoul of Deputy U. S. Marshall Candace Maldonado, but he considered it couldn't hurt to drive by at a normal speed and see what there was to see.

What remained of the station itself was charred black. The entire property was cordoned off in more yellow tape. The Marshals' van and sedan were parked off to the side and he could see the crew in jumpsuits, engaged in various activities around the premises.

He didn't see Bartolli but did catch a glimpse of Maldonado, standing over a crew member who was squatting down next to the remains of a gasoline pump. There were still a handful of curious pedestrians passing and stopping to peer in at the wreckage. Frank could swear he still smelled the carbon odors from the fire.

He was more familiar with the smells of burned material—and flesh—than he would have liked.

He drove down the street, turned around and drove past one more time, giving the scene a quick look as he passed. He wasn't quite sure why he had wanted to do this. It wasn't his problem to begin with, and he wasn't sure what was to be gained from looking at it in any case. He was just following some intangible urge, he decided.

Maybe just killing time. This place was getting to him and he needed to stay busy until he left tomorrow morning.

So what next?

Maybe he could rent a movie back at his motel room, then grab some dinner. Maybe see if Francis would like him to drop by one last time tonight. His mind wandered to their dinner together the previous night. He randomly revisited the meal, their conversation, the house…

What suddenly struck him was such a minor detail, but all at once it loomed large.

The things the mind will do, Frank mused, if you leave it alone. The connections it can come up with.

He knew what he'd be doing tonight.

* * * *

"Hey, Frank, come on in." Francis met him at the door with a beer can in his left hand and extended his right to shake.

"Just wanted to come by and say goodbye if you have a few minutes."

"Sure, sure! Come on in." Francis shook the can in his hand. It made a shallow sloshing sound. "I was just going to refresh this. Can I offer you one?"

Frank stepped into the house. "Actually, if you've got any coffee, that sounds better to me."

Francis took another look at the beer can in his hand. "You know, that actually sounds like a better idea. I'm afraid I've been hitting the sauce a bit too much the past few days. Let me go toss this and put up a pot for us. Make yourself at home." He gestured into the living room. "I'll be right back."

Frank found his way back to the same chair he had occupied the previous night and picked up the Lafferty College yearbook from where it still sat on the coffee table. In retrospect, he was surprised it had been left there on the table the past few days.

That had been a mistake on Francis's part.

He paged through to a particular section and scanned several of the pages. He looked up as Francis returned and sat down once again on the couch across from him.

"Coffee'll be ready shortly. So when is your flight out?"

"Tomorrow evening. I'll be leaving in the morning. A couple hours' drive to the airport."

Francis nodded. "I guess you had something of a busman's holiday here, didn't you? I mean, with the deaths and all. Did it make you feel right at home?"

Frank shrugged with a smile. "Getting back home to work is going to seem pretty pedestrian after all the stuff going on around here."

"Pretty insane, all right. Did you find out anything else about that guy from the lodge, what might have happened to him?"

"From what the deputy told me, I guess it's all right to tell you. It looks as if it was an accidental shooting. Some kid taking potshots off a bridge late at night. One of them hit that guy."

Francis' eyes widened for a moment. "You're kidding!"

"They're looking into a couple of local kids. Lyle and Lem, I think were their names?"

Francis nodded. "Lloyd Crimmins' kids. I know them. Come to think of it, Lyle's gotten in trouble for shooting at stuff with his air rifle now and then. Broke a few windows more than once. There were like four people in my store repairing their windows one day and grousing about it."

"This was a twenty-two. Sounds like they're really into their guns at that house."

Francis nodded. "Lots of hunters and such around here. I stock some rifles and shotguns and ammunition. I've sold a couple of guns to Lloyd and his boys. They go on a lot of hunting trips."

"I heard something about Lloyd coming back from the Gulf War a little messed up?"

"I've heard the stories too. I've known Lloyd for many years. He's basically a good guy. Something sure seems to have happened to him while he was away. I mean, it's not like he's nuts or anything. He's just become withdrawn in recent years. The kids, though…they're kind of sketchy. Their mom's not around anymore and Lloyd, well, I don't think he's doing much in the way of parenting or discipline."

"The mom died?"

"No, she just left town one day a year or so ago. I think she just couldn't take that gang anymore."

"So the boys are, what, teenagers?"

"Yeah. I'm not sure of their exact ages. Lem's the younger one, he's maybe fourteen? Lyle's about sixteen or seventeen, I'd guess."

"It would seem one of them is the prime suspect in the shooting at this point. Do me a favor and don't spread that around. I have a feeling the whole story will be coming out soon enough anyway."

Francis held his hands in the air with a smile. "Mum's the word from here." There came a series of beeps from the kitchen. Francis stood up. "Coffee's done. Be right back. You take anything in yours?"

"Black," said Frank.

"I should have figured. In the stories, cops always take it black."

"For once the stories get it right."

Frank sat back in the chair and folded his arms. He considered exactly how he wanted to broach the next subject. He was still in that pose when Francis returned with two mugs and placed one on the table in front of Frank.

"I'm glad you came here for Muriel," Francis said as he sat back down.

"Me too. Hey, remember we were talking about your college days and all?"

"Sure. What about 'em?"

Frank picked up the yearbook and paged through it. He looked casual but there was something he was particularly looking for.

"Was this guy a particular friend of yours?" He opened the book and pointed to a photo. Francis leaned over and looked.

"Oh yeah. I knew Pat, sure. Why?"

"You said a couple of guys you knew in school came from families of mobsters, I think you called them. Was this Pat Fine one of them?"

Francis did not answer for a long beat. He just stared first at the book and then up at Frank.

"Why are you asking, Frank?"

"Kind of a coincidence. Just before Ralph Watkins moved here, there was a guy in Boston who turned state's evidence against a prominent organized crime figure named Pat Fine. It says here your friend was from the Boston area. I'm wondering if they were related. If possibly your friend was the son of the other Pat Fine."

"I suppose it's possible."

"Come on, Francis. This guy was a friend of yours, wasn't he? You knew the background he was coming out of, didn't you? Why so coy all of a sudden?"

Francis looked down at his coffee cup and said nothing.

"Let me just come out and say all of this. You've been visibly troubled for the past couple of days. I thought that was natural because of the loss of your wife. But then I got to thinking about it. You seemed better to me the night of the wake. You looked much worse the morning of the burial. That was after word of Ralph Watkins' death had spread. That afternoon you met with Father McNulty for something that seemed to be serious. I'm thinking you suddenly felt guilty about something, that you had something to share in the confessional. Tell me if I'm way off base here, Francis."

Francis still said nothing, just stared at his coffee cup.

"You told me last night that you hadn't had any contact with any of your old college buddies in many years. I'm thinking that's not quite true. I'm thinking you had a conversation with your old friend

Pat Fine recently. I'm thinking something in that conversation tipped him off to the fact that there might be someone here in Easton that would be of special interest to his family. Both his 'families' actually. Tell me I'm wrong, Francis. Please, tell me I'm wrong, and I'll stop right there."

Francis finally looked up and with a sinking feeling, Frank understood that he was not wrong.

"You're thinking it's your fault that the guy who called himself Barry Fields came to town, and that he killed Ralph."

Francis shook his head and whispered, "Damn." A tear swelled in the inner corner of one eye.

"I do not want this to be right, but I'm getting the feeling it is."

Francis nodded his head.

"Why? How did you figure out who Ralph was and how did you decide to do this?"

"Muriel had him figured out. Well, not completely, but she had worked out he was from around Boston, a few other things about him. He said he was here to forget something and just start his life over new. We all respected that. We made some private jokes, when he wasn't around, about Witness Protection, but they were just jokes. Muriel didn't mean any harm. She was just curious. You know how she was. She was trying to figure out how to help him."

"So Muriel suspected who he really was?"

"She didn't have a real name or the exact circumstances or anything like that. But I think she knew enough to make Ralph a little uncomfortable. He was beginning to shy away from her. Politely, but it seemed clear he was avoiding her."

"I'm not quite sure I understand. When did you call your friend about Ralph? Why did you do it?"

Francis stared intently at Frank. "I called Pat the night that Muriel died. I was convinced that Ralph had killed her."

The rest of the story took some time to come out with any kind of clarity. Frank was once again going over it with Francis and was finally sipping some of the coffee in his mug.

"I still don't quite get it. You came home from work and found Muriel on the ground outside at the foot of the ladder. How did you conclude that Ralph was responsible?"

"Hell, Frank, I was in shock. You can imagine. Coming home to find the woman you love…lying there?"

"I can't imagine. That would be horrible." Frank had seen his share of horrors, things that stretched the capacity of the human mind and heart, but he honestly could not imagine himself in a scenario of that kind.

"I was nuts. I called 911. I tried CPR, as well as I know it anyhow. I hoped against hope she wasn't really dead. I desperately prayed that she was still alive somehow."

"I don't blame you."

"The cops and EMTs arrived right away and pronounced her dead. There was a big fuss and they took her away and told me there was nothing else I could do that night. After a while I told everyone that I'd be okay and they could leave me. Then I really started going crazy. I poured myself a couple of stiff drinks. All I could think of was that none of this made any sense.

"First, I felt guilty as hell. She had been nagging me to go up and get that bird's nest and I was all caught up in stuff at work and told her I'd get to it soon enough. It was my fault that she had gone up there. Then I started thinking that it didn't make any sense that she would have done that. She would have waited for someone to be here to hold the ladder for her and help her. Who could that have been? I started building this whole story. It had to have been Ralph. He had come by and innocently volunteered to help her and then knocked her off the ladder. The more I thought about it, and the more I drank, the more sense it all made. Around one in the morning, I looked up Pat Fine and made the call. I didn't know who Ralph really could be but I figured he was some kind of witness-protection type from Boston, and I had a suspicion Pat was connected these days. I just was so full of grief that I wanted to get back at him."

"You never told the police any of your suspicions then."

"What was I going to tell them? What proof would there have been?"

"Maybe Ralph's fingerprints on the ladder?"

"I never thought of that. Anyway, by the next morning I sure wasn't going to say anything. Not if I had set in motion what I thought I had."

"You must have had misgivings the next day. Second thoughts."

"I woke up with a terrible sense of loss of Muriel. The hangover didn't help that any. I didn't give the rest of it much thought that next day. When I finally did, it all seemed foggy and unreal. I kinda remembered making the call to Pat but didn't even believe that it had any effect. He probably thought I was crazy with grief and drunk when we talked. He likely didn't take me seriously."

"You didn't make any effort to call off anything you might have put into play?"

"No. I figured that at worst it was a bell I couldn't un-ring at that point, but that far more likely, nothing would come of it anyway."

"What did Pat say to you when you told him that story?"

"I don't remember much. He was pretty noncommittal. I did wake him up; it was pretty early in the morning in Boston."

"He didn't let on that he might be as connected as you suspected? To his father's organization, I mean."

"No, I don't remember him ever saying anything definite about that. He probably made some disclaimers in fact. I would have expected that. The whole thing seemed so stupid and embarrassing to me later."

"And then the morning of the burial, you found out that Ralph was killed in a dubious accident."

"Dubious is the word." Francis shook his head. "The worst part? I'm not so sure I really believe he did it any more...killed Muriel I mean. Maybe after all it was just a stupid accident."

It seemed a very long time that they sat in silence, drinking from their mugs, not even looking at one another. Somewhere in Francis's house, a clock ticked. In the pall of the house the ticks sounded like crashes.

Finally Francis spoke softly.

"I'm going to turn myself in tomorrow."

"Did the Padre advise you to do that?"

"Not in so many words. He told me I should follow my conscience. He suggested it might be one course of action."

Frank did not answer.

"I don't know if I can live with myself if I don't, Frank."

"I understand. You have to do what you think is right."

"What if you were in my place, what would you do?"

"Oh damn, I wish you wouldn't ask me something like that. But just some things to think about."

"Okay."

"I'm pretty sure that Ralph really was a guy who worked for the Boston mob. If he's who I think he was, he wasn't a good guy by any means. He did a lot of bad stuff in his life. I'm talking really bad stuff. He didn't turn on his employers until someone took out his family. And then he went state's evidence and saved his own neck. That's one thing."

"Are you trying to say he got what he deserved? How could he have deserved to die like that?"

"No, that's not what I'm saying, not at all. I'm saying that he had already set things in motion and for all we know, this is how it had to end for him. Some people would call it karma. Maybe it seems harsh, but that's my perspective from what I do every day. He lived by the sword and he died by the sword."

Francis didn't seem to have anything to say to that so Frank continued.

"Another thing is, you don't know what happened or how the wise guys found him. I think that by a very strange coincidence, Ralph sent Pat Fine, the father, to Federal prison. He put a lot of Fine's organization on law enforcement radar. Tracking Ralph down and making him pay had to be high on their must-do list. They were already looking for him, and those guys are pretty smart and thorough. You don't know if calling your old friend had any effect or not. You can't be sure your pal was even in his father's business. A lot of that generation, if their parents were in the organization, they wanted to get their kids out of that, into legitimacy. You were in the bag when you called him and woke him up at an ungodly hour, and you don't know whether he even took you seriously. The bottom line, Francis, is that you don't really know if you did anything at all. You don't know if you have any responsibility in this whatsoever."

Francis nodded somberly. "Father McNulty said some of the same things."

"On top of that, Federal Marshals are in town. They've taken over the investigation. They're not happy. The Witness Security Program has never lost a single relocated witness that played by the rules, and these people don't want to become the first, so there's a certain wishful thinking, let's say, that this turns out to be a tragic accident and nothing more. The Sheriff is ticked off at the outsiders coming in, taking over his territory and bringing this catastrophe down upon him, and he's just going to want to see this swept under the rug too. I'm not saying that anyone wants to actively obscure the true story of what may have happened, or necessarily plans to tell any lies. I'm simply saying that there likely isn't going to be any high profile legal action coming out of it. Anything that does result is going to be on the down low, and probably won't involve highly visible prosecutions. So if you feel the right thing is to tell your story, by all means, do so. I am not telling you what to do or not do. But be aware of the context in which your story's going to be received. Be ready to have it met with some skepticism."

Francis digested all of that quietly.

"One further thing. If you do come forward on this, I'd suggest you talk to Deputy Lee Maravich. And I strongly suggest that you do NOT mention my name in any of this."

"Do you think they're going to think I'm crazy?"

"Maravich won't. Someone might try to make YOU think you are. But that's not why you want to come forward, is it?"

Francis simply shook his head.

Frank thought about the need to remove the burden of guilt, what power it could hold. His past few days, he realized, had been filled with it.

He thought about Kieran McNulty, carrying so much, not just in his role as a father confessor but also as a twelve-step sponsor. He couldn't imagine shouldering that much of a burden of confidentiality.

"You know what's funny?" Francis said quietly.

"No, what?"

"Pat called me Frank. That's how he remembered me. I said 'This is Francis Lansdowne' and he said, 'Hey, Frank! What's up?' It was like I was back in the old school days, like all the years in between had never happened. I was Frank again."

"So here we are. Two Franks."

"That's what Muriel used to say. She had a fondness for Franks. She'd kid me when she'd refer to you, you were the Other Frank."

"At least she didn't call you the other one." Frank laughed despite himself. "Waiter, two Franks, please."

Francis actually cracked a weak smile. "And hold the mustard."

SEVEN

Frank had dropped his bag into the trunk of the rental car and closed it when he saw Lee Maravich, in uniform, standing in front of his car, arms folded across his chest.

"Morning. I was hoping I'd catch you before you left."

"Don't they ever give you a day off, Deputy?"

"They got me on a lot of overtime this week, what with all that's been going on. My wife's not happy that I couldn't join her at church this morning."

"I'll bet she'll be less unhappy when that overtime pay comes in your envelope."

"Good point. I have to believe you're happy to be getting away from all this mess and leaving it to us."

"You keep telling me this isn't how things usually are around here, but I'm beginning to have my doubts. I'm looking forward to returning to the usual straightforward murders and muggings back home."

Maravich laughed. "Honest to God, this is usually a quiet town, downright boring."

"How are things working out with the shooting?"

"We got prints off of Barry Fields and sent them out to the FBI's database. So far nothing's come back. We're still trying for an ID of some kind. His company's a dead end and so far there aren't any other viable leads such as next of kin or anything like that. The actual shooting, pretty much what we expected. The ballistics matched up to Lemuel Crimmins' gun. The other evidence played out the same way: the shoe print, the fingerprints, the whole nine yards. We found a witness who saw the father Lloyd's pickup truck on the divided overpass highway that night. Lem's pretty much owned up to being out there, taking potshots at passing cars for a couple nights. He must have realized that he hit Fields. It seems he picked up and took off in a hurry right after that."

"He's just a kid, right?"

"Not even fifteen."

"Pretty messed up. His life's never going to be the same."

"I have to say, some of us saw it coming. But you're right, it's a shame. Maybe this will serve as a wakeup call for Lloyd. Maybe he'll get some help for himself, and maybe at least Lyle's still got a chance."

"Redemption," Frank muttered. There seemed to be a lot of people seeking it or needing it here this week.

"Speaking of redemption, I had a visit earlier this morning from Francis Lansdowne." Maravich raised his eyebrows.

"Really."

"He told me quite a story. I have a feeling you might know something about it already."

"I'm just a visitor, getting ready to go home."

"Uh-huh. He claims he made a phone call that might have set things in motion, Barry Fields and the fire and all."

"And why would he do that, exactly?"

"He claims that he thought Ralph might have killed Muriel." Maravich eyed Frank carefully.

"Why would Ralph kill Muriel?"

"Because he thinks that Muriel had figured out who Ralph really was."

"Really. Do you put any stock in that?"

"Can't say as I do. The story he told me is pretty convoluted. A lot of ifs and maybes. I'm not even sure how we can look into it. On top of that, it's a big stretch for me to believe that Ralph Watkins would have killed Muriel Lansdowne. Even Francis wasn't sure he really believed it in the end."

"And what does Sheriff Riculla think of it?"

"I haven't broached it with him as yet. He gets to sleep in late this morning and come in in the afternoon. I doubt he'll welcome this development. I'm not yet sure what I'm going to tell him—or not."

"What about the Marshals? Are they still around?"

"I think they cleared out last night or earlier today. I don't see their vehicles here." They both glanced around at the basically empty parking lot. "The Bobbsey Twins stopped in at the station last night for another high level get together with Rick Riculla."

"The Bobbsey Twins. Good name for them."

"I have still not been privy to any of those conferences. I have a feeling he's going to give us the word later today or tomorrow."

"You're thinking that the powers that be want this case closed."

"I am thinking that, yes."

"But you don't."

"I do not. But I'm not sure what my options are at this point."

"You're a good cop, Lee. You're going to do the right thing, but you also know exactly what you're up against."

"To be honest, right now I'm not sure what I think I ought to do."

"Hey, I've told you, I hate it when Federal or state authorities come in and step on my business, and I really hate it when wise guy types come in from out of town to foul my nest. We've got a hard enough job under normal circumstances, without all this outside nonsense. I definitely get it. And when something's unsettled, it stays up there in my head as well. I get all that, I really do."

Maravich nodded solemnly. "But you gotta know when to hold 'em and when to fold 'em."

"Exactly." Frank put his hand out. "Drop me a line sometime, let me know how you came out of all this."

Maravich shook his hand firmly. "I'll do that, Detective. Thanks for the conversations."

"It's been a pleasure, Lee."

"Same here. Safe journey home. Vaya con Dios, as we say back in Texas."

"It's funny, there's something the Padre said to me."

"Which was?"

"Something to the effect that it's never a question of whether God's with you but whether you're with God. Or maybe that's just how I interpreted it."

"Yeah, that sounds like the Padre all right. Eternal optimist, huh?"

"Frankly, Lee, unless he's a vigilante at heart, I'm not seeing the hand of God very much in the proceedings of this week."

Maravich nodded slowly and somberly. "Hard to be like the Padre if you're a cop."

Frank traced a benediction in the air. "Amen to that, brother."

* * * *

Frank drove along the highway, his head still buzzing with all the elements of the crazy story in which he had lived for the past few days. Protected Federal witness in a new identity. Mob hit man. Murder made to look like a fluke accidental death. In a bizarre twist, a fluke accidental death that looked like a murder.

Possibly—just possibly—his ex-wife, playing detective, getting herself killed.

A blooming cover-up by Federal authorities with the coerced complicity of the local Sheriff.

The taste it all left in his mouth was at least as bad as anything he had ever experienced in Personal Crimes.

Before he knew it, the hours had slipped away, the secondary road had brought him to the Interstate, and he was on the exit ramp for the airport. He hardly remembered any of it.

* * * *

It was over two weeks later when the mail cart passed through the unit and the duty officer dropped his mail on his desk. There was a large manila envelope on top, hand lettered with a familiar return address. He ripped it open and pulled out a folded up section from a Midwestern newspaper. A yellow Post-It note was stuck onto the first page with a two-word printed message in the same hand as the address: THERE'S MORE.

Lee Maravich. Frank shook his head and smiled.

He opened it up and read the headline to the article:

EXISTENCE OF A PROTECTED MOB
WITNESS SHOCKS A SMALL TOWN

The muddled mystery that has baffled a small town for the past ten days seems to finally be coming to a head with new official disclosures.

A spokesperson for the U.S. Marshals Service today confirmed that a man who died in a service station fire last week in the township of Easton had in fact been living under an assumed identity as part of the Federal Witness Security Program.

Raymond Lawrence "Larry" Warnecke, a longtime member of New England organized crime, whose crucial prosecution testimony cemented the case against mob boss Pat Fine, was relocated to Easton three years ago and was living under the assumed identity of Ralph Leonard Watkins, the proprietor of Ralph's Automotive Services.

Deputy U.S. Marshal Candace Maldonado affirmed Warnecke's true identity and said that he had been established in the area with the knowledge, consent and cooperation of local law enforcement.

Some questions had been raised, Maldonado further explained, regarding the circumstances around Warnecke's death, but these had been carefully and thoroughly investigated and the Marshals Service was now completely satisfied that the tragic explosion and fire were the result of an accident. She pointed out that the U.S. Marshals Service has an unblemished record of protection of its charges when they have cooperated with the requirements of the program, and that this case was no exception.

Freeman County Sheriff Richard Riculla confirmed Maldonado's statement, including that he had been made aware of Warnecke's true identity and had been consulted prior to the relocation, but declined to expand upon that.

Frank shook his head as he continued to read the remainder of the article. There was no mention of Barry Fields' presence or death. It was as if the question of Fields' possible involvement in the death of Ralph Watkins was never even a consideration. He could imagine Lee Maravich's reaction to all this. He wondered what the "more" promised by the sticky-note could be.

It wasn't long before his questions were answered.

Later that same day Frank received a call.

"Detective Vandegraf, this is FBI Special Agent Gary Hedges. Possibly you remember me."

"Agent Hedges. Of course I do. The Shumer case."

"I happen to be in town right now. Might I be able to meet with you?"

"As a matter of fact, I'm about to grab some lunch. Can you join me?"

"Actually, this is business and I'm on a deadline. How about I bring us up some sandwiches, might there be somewhere private we can talk there?"

Frank was able to commandeer an interview room, basically a bare-walled chamber badly in need of a paint job with nothing but a metal table and chairs, and he apologized for the Spartan amenities. Hedges waved it off. He was a tall, broad-shouldered man and looked to have aged considerably since the last time they had met a couple of years previously.

Hedges came bearing a large paper bag and a briefcase. They sat and Hedges handed him a wrapped sandwich and a container of coffee. "Hope you don't mind if we eat while we talk. I'm on a flight in a few hours and I need to make every minute count. Nice place you suggested for the grub, by the way. The Reubens look good."

"Their coffee is better than ours too," Frank said happily. As Feds went, Hedges was about as decent as they came, and more than a little unorthodox at times. Generally Personal Crimes was not delighted to deal with the Bureau, but a little bit of good personal history went a long way. "Appreciate this. So what can I do for you, Agent?"

"Call me Gary, okay?" Somehow Hedges managed to simultaneously unwrap his sandwich while snapping open his briefcase and removing a manila folder, which he slid across the table to Frank. He was definitely not your stereotypical Bureau agent, Frank mused. But he had learned that the guy's quirkiness masked an almost scary sharpness and tenacity. Everything was to a purpose.

"Check out the guy in this file. Look familiar to you?" he said as he bit into the Reuben.

Frank opened the file and stared at two four-by-five inch photographs clipped to a typed report with a very familiar format.

"This looks like Artie Burns."

Hedges took another bite, put down the sandwich, and simply nodded.

Frank scrutinized the face in the photos. "He looks a little different in these photos, the hair and the clean shaven face, and he's a bit younger, but I'd say it's him, sure."

"I believe you also know him by another name as well."

"You don't mean…?"

"Barry Fields?"

Now it was Frank's turn to simply stare. It made sense, of course. It was just a surprise to hear anyone else accepting it.

Hedges smiled and pointed to the report. "I don't think it will come as any surprise to you, neither of those is his real name. Or was."

"They must have run a fingerprint check," Frank said. "The Sheriff's Department in Easton."

"IAFIS. You can read the report right there."

Frank scanned the stapled sheets. The Bureau's Integrated Automated Fingerprint Identification System—IAFIS—was the largest criminal fingerprint base in the world, and also included millions of civil prints. It was available to law enforcement throughout the country. Of course someone would have sent a set of Fields's prints to the database for comparison.

"Mitchell Gravell?" Frank read the name off the page.

"That's how we've got him in the system."

"How did you happen to make the connection and jump on this? I mean, YOU, personally?"

"Well, now, that's an interesting story. I was contacted by a Sheriff's Deputy from out there in Freeman County. He asked for me specifically."

"Let me guess. Lee Maravich."

Hedges' manner turned serious. "This is strictly between you and me now." Frank nodded in agreement. "We had a most interesting conversation, let me tell you."

"Unbelievable. I only briefly mentioned you in passing when we were talking. Lee's a sharp cookie."

"He provided me with enough to run with. I started retracing some of the other accidents we suspected were hit jobs. So far I can't definitely establish this guy's presence at the time and place of any of them, but there are some interesting coincidences that are turning up. They're still long shots but with some more hard work, we might just start to make some inroads on those connections. This guy's good. Or he was. He avoided trouble. But everybody makes a mistake sooner or later."

Frank continued to read over the report sheets. "Vagrancy in some small town in Eastern Shore Maryland? You gotta be kidding me. That's his entire rap sheet?"

"Something must have gone bad and he was trying to make it back to his home base, which we believe to be New England. A fluke of luck. Nobody would ever have picked up on this if he hadn't gotten himself killed. He would have been buried in the cracks of the system forever."

"So what do you need from me?"

Hedges smiled.

"I need you to help me with the one case I think I can definitely pin on our friend here and begin to trace it back to the Organization. Larry Warnecke. I believe you know the name?"

"I was led to believe that case has been closed by the Marshals."

"Yes, well…they would LIKE for that case to be closed. The Bureau feels a little differently about it."

Frank envisioned a very, *very* unhappy Deputy Marshall Maldonado. The image was not entirely unpleasant to him. But it had its downside.

"You're dropping me right into the middle of an interagency squabble, it sounds like."

Hedges put up a hand. "Your name is never even going to come up in this. Officially, all we are discussing here today is the case we originally conferred on, the Lon Shumer murder. The entire reason I'm here is to confer on background and information on your case, which I hope we can do in detail. And I think you can look forward to our unearthing considerably more on that before we are finished. But on this other matter…"

Hedges paused to consider his words. "Just between you and me and nobody else. You were there. Maybe you feel that justice has not been served, as does another individual who shall also remain unnamed."

Frank shook his head. "You could get Lee in a hell of a lot of trouble, Gary. And me too."

"Do me a favor, Frank. Just tell me what you know? I'm going to keep both your names totally out of this, you have my solemn word, and I hope we've got sufficient history that that means something to you. But I need to have some plausible springboard from which to launch my investigation."

He reached over his sandwich into the briefcase and pulled out a pencil and a notebook. "No recordings. All handwritten. We all want the same thing here. There're a lot of wise guys I've been after who think they've gotten away scot-free with all kinds of mischief, and I want them in the worst way. There's potential here for us to take down a lot of them, to clear a lot of open cases we thought were hopeless for once and for all. Please, help me out."

Frank considered for a long moment and weighed the pros and cons. Lee Maravich had shown some guts in contacting Hedges. It was clear the truth meant a lot to him in the scheme of things. He couldn't leave him hanging out on that limb by himself.

But he didn't have to tell it all. He never mentioned anything about Francis.

EIGHT

It was two days later, as he was grabbing his car keys and preparing to head out the door on a fresh call, when Frank's old-style flip cell phone started buzzing in his pocket. He fished it out and answered it, gruff and a bit impatient. "Frank Vandegraf."

"Lee Maravich here."

"Lee! What's up?" Frank dropped his keys back on the desk and plopped himself into his chair. The murder call could wait a couple of minutes, he reflected. Everybody was already dead there. Nobody was going anywhere.

"Got a minute?"

"Why not? You seem to be trying to get us both in a heap of trouble these days."

"Listen to you. 'Heap of trouble'? That your idea of sounding like a Texas boy?"

"Seriously, Lee. Special Agent Hedges came into town the other day, just to talk with me about all sorts of things. I'm sure you're the one who put him up to that. I'm amazed you remembered his name. I only mentioned him once."

"Sometimes, I'm not such a bad cop, Frank."

"So, to what do I owe the honor of this call?"

"I promised I'd keep you in the loop. Thought you'd be interested in recent developments."

"Go ahead."

"I found reason to go back and check a few things around Francis Lansdowne's house. Happened to pull some prints off his ladder. Even with it having been touched and moved around some more in the past couple weeks, would it surprise you to learn that it held a few fingerprints belonging to that Warnecke fellow, or should I say Ralph Watkins? On top of that, Francis told me there was never a time in his memory that Ralph had ever been at his house, so that led from one thing to another."

"How did you get the Sheriff to go along with that one?"

"Um, I sort of didn't. It happened to come up on a day while Rick

Riculla was on a fishing trip. Just sort of a coincidence."

"Uh huh. Astounding coincidence. And how did Sheriff Riculla react when he found out you had done that?"

"I put the whole thing together and presented it to him as a *fait accompli*. Did you know Texas boys said stuff like that, '*fait accompli*'?"

"I do now."

"Anyway, I had a chance to think it out and suggest a way he could announce all this and make himself look real good, so he kinda forgave me."

"Better to beg for forgiveness than to ask for permission," Frank recited.

"Rule to live by. Heard that a bit in my stint in Texas. Anyhow, by another strange coincidence, this all went down just as Special Agent Hedges arrived and began his own investigation into the death of Watkins—I mean Warnecke. Whoever."

"For a man who doesn't believe in coincidences, you are up to your ears in them all of a sudden."

"Funny thing, isn't it? Well, that was another matter that came up to irritate Rick Riculla, and I sorta suggested a way to make lemonade out of all these lemons falling on his head."

"What's the bottom line on all this? Is Francis going to be involved in any of it?"

"Nope. I never mentioned his little confession to the Sheriff or anybody else. Kinda saw no reason to. As far as anybody else knows, the evidence that Warnecke might have killed Muriel came as a shock to Francis. Your bottom line is that Warnecke crossed the line and committed a murder, and now there's reason to believe he wasn't exactly toeing the line to begin with. Maybe he cut a few other corners and broke a few other laws while he was living in Easton. There's sufficient doubt so that they can paint him as a rogue in the Program. The Marshals can make a case that their Witness Security Program record is still unblemished in cases where the subject played by the rules, so they are now publicly cooperating with the FBI to establish the truth about Barry Fields and the death of Larry Warnecke."

"Sounds too neat to be for real."

"So far, so good, Frank. Riculla's on board and it might just play out for the best. He's no fan of the Bobbsey Twins since they originally dropped this whole Witness Protection thing in his lap, and he's kinda pleased that in private they're gnashing their teeth over these developments. The Sheriff does like his payback."

"I'm glad Francis can be kept out of this."

"No need to bring him in. There're only three of us, including Francis himself, who know the real story about his involvement, and none of us seem predisposed to telling it."

Four, thought Frank, but the Padre wasn't about to say anything either.

Lee Maravich, apparently nowhere near the straight arrow he had presumed, continued to surprise him. He was beginning to remind Frank of some of the hard-boiled protagonists in the noir crime dramas Muriel loved: principled but starkly realistic guys who weren't beyond bending a rule to see real justice done.

"It looks as if Hedges might be tracing that Fields character back to some other hits as well," Frank said, "including our cold case on Lon Shumer. We might yet close that one, even if we don't end up with any official credit, which is a real possibility. Hedges is a good man in my estimation, but the Feds are great at hogging the spotlight. What we might be able to take from this is some closure anyway, knowing that our instincts were right, and that the killers didn't get away after all."

"You and I both know we might not get out of this exactly how we'd like to, right?"

"Seldom do, Lee, in my experience."

"Mine as well, Frank, but let's hope for the best. Well, just thought I'd bring you up to speed. And fact be known, I do think everything's going to turn out just fine. Keep your fingers crossed. The game's afoot."

"Damn, do they say that in Texas too?"

"Picked that up from some English guy somewhere, as I recall."

"Keep in touch, Deputy. It's been a pleasure working—well, officially not working–with you. Watch your back."

"Vaya con Dios, Detective. Hasta la vista."

Frank hung up and reached for his car keys once again.

It was better than he had expected, if not as good as he had hoped.

Strangely, he felt a little lighter as he stood up and headed for the door. In the corridor, he passed a glum-looking Marlon Morrison, who shot him an odd look.

"Hey, what the devil are you so happy about all of a sudden, Frank?" He moved on without waiting for a reply, grumbling to himself beneath labored breath.

Frank realized he must be smiling, and he hadn't done much of that in the past few days.

As good a time to move on as ever.

ABOUT THE AUTHOR

Tony Gleeson, an inveterate fan of jazz and classic mysteries, is a writer, illustrator and graphic designer. He lives with his wife Anne and their cats, Django and Mingus, in Los Angeles, California.

www.ingramcontent.com/pod-product-compliance
Lightning Source LLC
Chambersburg PA
CBHW020638180626
46816CB00003B/1021